Scorching Hot Threesomes 3

Darren G. Burton

Contents

Kitty Bang Bang

Jeff dove underwater and skimmed between two submerged, barnacle-encrusted boulders. He pursued a large tropical fish. He didn't know what type of fish it was, but it was very pretty in its shades of white, red, yellow and blue. The fish was way too fast for him and, with a powerful flick of its tail fin, shot out to sea like a bullet. Jeff made for the surface some ten feet above and immediately blew the water from his snorkel as he broke into the sunlight. He spat out the mouthpiece and sucked in several quick and deep breaths. He coughed up some seawater that had lodged in his throat and did a pirouette in the water, taking in the scenery.

He was diving around a rocky headland in water that was about twenty feet deep. The day was fine and clear, the morning sun already quite high in the sky and burning down on the resort that was nestled amid palms just off the beach. The water shimmered as a light breeze rippled across it. Swimmers were everywhere, as well as several kayaks, catamarans and a few speedboats heading towards the outer reef. The pristine beach was dotted with a myriad of colors as tourists crowded the sand.

Jamming the mouthpiece between his lips once more, Jeff lowered his face into the water and kicked lazily around the headland, propelling himself with only his fins. A school of fish darted left and right below him. Jeff reached down with a hand and they scattered in all directions before regrouping further away from him.

Taking a deep breath he kicked down towards the bottom, equalizing the building pressure in his ears by pinching his nose and trying to exhale through his nostrils. His ears popped and the pain vanished instantly. He weaved through some rocks and under an overhang, making his way around to the beach on the other side of the headland. When his lungs protested and screamed for air, he quickly rose to the surface and took a deep breath.

As he pushed his mask up onto his forehead and squinted against the glare, he saw a thin red protrusion snaking left and right. Behind the snorkel two cheeks of a cute female bum bobbed up and down in the water, the succulent flesh clad in a white bikini bottom.

Jeff saw no one with the lone swimmer. Curious, he replaced his face mask, sucked the snorkel between his lips and kicked hard in the direction of the woman, catching up to her in thirty seconds. When he was within ten feet of her he slowed down and casually followed her into shore. She looked young and slim from behind and she moved with all the grace of someone very comfortable in water.

She stopped and hovered above some rocks a few metres from shore. Jeff casually kicked over to her, pretending to study the sea bed. When she saw him she broke the surface. Jeff did likewise and simultaneously they spat out their snorkels and raised their masks so they could make unimpeded eye contact.

The girl looked early twenties, was a brunette and she had a very pretty face. She smiled a genuine and friendly smile.

"Hi," she said brightly. "Were you following me?"

Jeff was momentarily caught off guard by her direct question.

"No...not really."

She raised an eyebrow. "Not really?" The smile never left her face.

"I'm Jeff," said Jeff, wanting to divert the topic of conversation as quickly as possible.

The young woman extended a hand. "My name's Katrina." Jeff took her hand in his and shook it once. The skin of her palm was soft and velvety. "Some people like to call me 'Kitten' or 'Kitty'. I actually prefer 'Kitty'."

Now Jeff grinned. "Kitty it is then." Behind her was a deserted expanse of beach, palm fronds waving lazily over the sand. "Are you here on holiday?"

Kitty nodded. "For ten days. I'm sharing a room with my sister and brother-in-law. We only got here last night. Are you on holiday too?"

Jeff shook his head. "I live here. I work part-time at the resort in PR."

"And the rest of the time you're enjoying all the spoils paradise has to offer." She shot him another smile, a mischievous glint in her eyes.

He replied, "Something like that."

She glanced at her diver's watch. "Listen, Jeff, I better head back. We're going on an excursion up in the mountains today. If you're not working later, why don't you join us for a drink at the pool bar around six this evening."

"Sure. I'm free. Look forward to it."

Kitty put her mask back on. "I better go. See you tonight."

"Enjoy the mountains," he said, but her head was already submerged in the water.

* * *

The setting sun was hovering just above the horizon line when Jeff made his way to the pool bar at six. The sea was painted in hues of deep red and orange.

Surprisingly the bar and pool area were fairly empty. Many patrons were probably off having dinner. Jeff spied Kitty sitting on a bar stool. She was dressed in a thin, translucent yellow dress and he could make out her white bikini beneath it. Sitting next to her was another brunette who looked to be a few years older, but equally as attractive. Jeff presumed it was Kitty's sister. To the right of the sibling was a thickset guy with a military-style haircut. He was busy nibbling on peanuts which he washed down with beer as the sisters engaged in animated conversation. When Kitty saw Jeff approaching, she waved him over.

"Jeff, this is my sister, Emily, and her husband, Mick." Jeff shook hands with both of them and took up a seat to the left of Kitty. "Would you like a beer?" she asked him. "Can we have another beer here, please, bartender?" A beer was immediately poured and placed in front of Jeff, foam oozing down the sides of the glass. "I'm glad you came, Jeff," she said with a smile.

He took a sip of beer. "How was the mountains?"

She nodded. "Great. Had a nice lunch up there, got some great photos of the views. It was stunning, actually." She downed some beer. "So, you don't have to work tonight?"

"Nope. Tomorrow I do, but not tonight."

Kitty placed a warm hand on his thigh and leaned in close. She said softly in his ear, "Do you mind if I hang out with you tonight? I think Emily and Mick would like the room to themselves for a few hours. If you know what I mean?"

Jeff smiled. "No problem. I'm sure you and I can find something to do together."

She looked into his eyes, smiling again. "Are you implying what I think you're implying?"

He returned her grin and sipped some more brew. "And what is it you think I'm implying?"

"The same thing that those two want to get up to tonight." She nodded over her shoulder.

"Could be. So, what do you think?"

"Do you come onto every tourist girl so quickly?"

"Only the ones I really fancy."

"I think I really like the sound of what you're suggesting. I could use a good-looking fuck buddy while I'm here." Kitty suddenly looked serious. "I presume you don't have a girlfriend or a wife?"

Jeff shook his head. "No, I don't."

"Like to keep yourself free to shag all the tourist hotties." She nodded and finished her beer. "I can understand that. If I worked here I'd probably be doing the same."

At that moment Emily and Mick announced their departure and

strolled off arm in arm back to the room. Kitty immediately moved her stool closer to Jeff's and placed her arms around him.

"Whereabouts do you live on this island?" she wanted to know.

"I have a small boutique apartment in the resort. Part of my remuneration package."

"Wanna got to your 'boutique' apartment?"

Jeff shook his head. "I have a better idea." He stood up and took her hand. "Come with me. The night is far too beautiful to be wasted indoors."

He led her down to the beach, where quite a few people milled around on the sand to watch the remnants of the sunset. Stars now speckled the darkening sky. Soon the moon would rise above the mountains in the east.

"Where are you taking me?" Kitty asked.

"To a spot where we can have some privacy."

"Should I have brought a towel?"

"You won't need one."

The further away from the resort they ventured, the fewer people they encountered. The beach soon ended at a rocky outcrop. Still holding her hand, Jeff led Kitty into the jungle and followed a path behind the headland, where they emerged into a small deserted cove on the other side.

"This is gorgeous," Kitty said and smiled. "Do you take all your conquests here?" She winked at him.

Jeff just shrugged nonchalantly. He had indeed taken a few women here and had his way with them.

Showing no inhibitions whatsoever, Kitty immediately shed her dress and went to work removing her bikini. Within twenty seconds she stood on the sand stark naked. Jeff feasted his hungry eyes on her lush curves and felt his mouth salivate. She sure was yummy, with hefty boobs, rounded hips and butt, and a snatch that was waxed completely smooth. It had been a week since he'd last fucked a tourist girl and he was feeling pretty randy.

"Well?" she said, standing with her hands on hips. "You can't give me what I need with your clothes on."

Jeff stripped out of his shirt and shorts, then tugged his underwear down his legs and kicked them onto the sand. His sizeable cock was already erect from perving on Kitty's naked flesh and she eyed it with excited anticipation.

Without a word they moved in close and kissed, hands all over each other, tongues lashing and lips slippery with saliva. Breathing came in heated bursts as their mutual desire escalated. Jeff searched out her cunt with the fingers of his right hand. He probed her entry, which was soaked with warm juice. Two fingers slipped easily inside her and she broke the kiss and groaned.

"I so need a fuck," she whispered hoarsely.

Jeff felt his cock being groped in the increasing darkness. It throbbed in her hand and she started to stroke it up and down between their bodies. More juice filled her pussy and Jeff probed deeper with his fingers. The feel of her juice against his hand gave him the insatiable urge to taste her.

Quickly he broke free of her and spread her dress out on the sand.

He flopped down onto his back and said, "Ride my face."

He watched as Kitty straddled him and lowered her steaming pussy onto his waiting mouth. The flesh of her mound and lips was warm and smooth on his face as he darted his eager tongue into her drenched passage. She tasted sweet and delicious and he greedily sucked the juice from her cunt and swallowed it.

Kitty moaned as she rocked back and forth on top of him, enjoying the sensation of his tongue inside her, his lips against hers. She grabbed a handful of his hair in her hand and ground herself down harder on his face. Jeff was finding it difficult to breath. His mouth was engulfed with the flesh of her cunt and his nose was squashed into her throbbing clitoris. He thrashed his tongue inside her as deeply as he could reach and tried to suck in a breath at the same time. Another tsunami of juice washed down her tunnel and into his open mouth. Jeff consumed every drop her pussy offered him and searched her passage for more. Kitty was starting to tremble on top of him now and he figured she was heading for a climax.

"Suck my clit," she demanded.

Jeff concentrated all his efforts on her clitoris. Kitty continued to squirm around on his face. Juice soaked his chin. His teeth bit into her clitoris and then he sucked it hard. She exploded on his face, her body quivering and shuddering as she howled in delight towards the heavens. Her orgasm was all over within a few seconds and she sat still. Jeff gently raised her off his face a little with his hands so he could catch his breath. He licked the juice from his lips and gratefully sucked in lungfuls of air.

She got off him then and kissed him, busily working her tongue into his mouth before using it to clean her juice from his face. Kitty kissed a line down his throat and onto his chest. She continued her downward travels until her tongue was lightly flicking over the head of his enraged cock.

"Suck it," he urged, his dick desperate for some attention.

Kitty didn't tease and make him wait. Her mouth immediately engulfed the head of his cock upon request and she sucked so hard that the intensity of it sent shivers all through his body. Jeff groaned up at the sky. His eyes were open and he was seeing stars as Kitty's tongue ran wet lines up and down his lengthy shaft. She kissed his balls and lashed them with her tongue before gently sucking one into her mouth. Then her tongue was on the move again until it reached the head of his cock once more. She licked it like an ice cream, then ran circles around it. A series of excited tingles swept through his loins.

"Take it back into your mouth," he suggested, and she did so.

As she sucked the head, Kitty expertly stroked his shaft with her right hand and fondled his sensitive testicles with the fingers of her left. Jeff watched her head bobbing up and down in the gloom, her dark hair falling across her face and obscuring her oral affections from his view. He didn't need to see what she was doing to him. He could feel every luscious touch of her lips and tongue on his member.

"You have a beautiful cock," she said, peering up at his face. Her tongue flicked over the head. "Nice and thick. Just the way I like my dicks. I can only imagine how good it's going to feel inside my horny kitty."

"You don't have to imagine," he told her. "You could sit on it right now."

She grinned. "In a minute." His cock vanished inside her mouth once again.

Kitty sucked him off for more than another minute. It was more like three or four. As much as Jeff wanted his dick buried deep inside her, he wasn't complaining. Her mouth felt fantastic and she gave incredible head. Very intense.

Finally, after what seemed like a marathon blow job, Kitty got into a crouch above him and lowered her throbbing cunt down his shaft, swallowing it inch by inch until her pussy lips were kissing his balls.

"Fuck that feels good!" he exclaimed as he absorbed the sensation of her tight, hot cunt wrapped snuggly around his cock. She was so wet and so obviously horny. It sounded like her pussy was sucking on his cock as she slowly rose and fell on his length.

"It feels even better inside me than I imagined," Kitty said softly, her eyes shut, a slight smile of satisfaction curling the corners of her mouth. "It's very filling. Just the way I like it."

"I want you to come on it."

"Don't worry. I'm sure I will. But first I just want to ride you slowly for a while and savor every beautiful inch of you. You just lay back and enjoy the ride."

Now Jeff grinned. "I think I can handle that."

Kitty rocked back and forth on him with the grace of a smooth ocean swell. He could feel her juice trickling down his balls and onto the dress beneath him. She was gloriously well-lubricated and her pussy was an absolute delight to be inside. She stroked up and down now, rising to the tip of his dick before plunging down his shaft and burying every inch of him inside her muff.

He reached out a hand and rubbed her clit with his thumb, watching her beautiful boobs bouncing in the light of the rising moon. A sheen of sweat had formed on her brow, the tropical night air warm and humid. She was totally gorgeous and he felt privileged to be fucking her in this romantic setting. One of her hands went behind her and he felt her long nails rake across his balls; an action that sent further tingles of pleasure spreading through his loins.

He urged, "Fuck me hard. I wanna see you come all over my big dick."

"Okay."

Kitty complied and increased her tempo until her pussy was pounding down his shaft and her cunt lips were smacking against his balls. She panted heavily, her rapid breathing matching the pace of her strokes. Jeff could see the tension building in her facial features. She was approaching another climax and he couldn't wait for his cock to make her come. That would be one orgasm inflicted by his mouth and one by his dick. It was an ego thing. But ego aside, he did like a woman enjoying the experience just as much as he did himself.

"That's it," he encouraged her. "Come on it. Come all over that big dick."

And she did, screaming as the intensity of the climax possessed her body and sent all her nerve endings into overdrive. She shivered on top of him, her thrusts becoming more awkward as her muscles momentarily seized up. Jeff helped her out by thrusting vigorously into her from below, slamming his cock to the very end of her tunnel and heightening her arousal. When she was done she collapsed into his arms, panting hard and trying to catch her breath. He wrapped his arms around her warm and sweating torso, enjoying the feel of those luscious mounds of breast flesh against his chest.

"That was...a really...good one," she managed to croak between ragged gasps for air.

He smiled. "I aim to please."

Her breathing was more under control now. "Any pussy on the end of your cock would be a happy pussy. If any of my girlfriends come here to party, I'm going to recommend they hook up with you."

A referral. Jeff liked the sound of that.

"Wanna do me doggy?" Kitty asked. "I like it doggy."

"So do I," he assured her and squirmed out from under her.

As Kitty got on all fours, Jeff positioned himself behind her, holding his erection horizontal and guiding the head towards her opening. He slipped all the way inside effortlessly and ground his cock head against the end of her tunnel.

"You have the best cock," she said as she grasped handfuls of her dress. "Give it to me hard and deep."

Jeff didn't disappoint. He drove his cock into her with relentless passion, spreading her wet lips around its wide girth and ramming the extremities of her sizzling passage. He had her hips gripped tightly in his hands as he fucked her. His balls swayed in their loose sack, slapping against her mound with every stroke. Her pussy got wetter by the second and he could sense juice running down the insides of her thighs.

"I love fucking you, Kitty," he told her enthusiastically.

"Fuck me then," she replied.

Jeff was a blur of motion as he slammed into her from the rear. Kitty howled and moaned and groaned and panted. He had her struggling for breath once more as his cock action rapidly built a third climax within her. She erupted all over his cock and thrust her ass backwards to meet his damaging strokes. Her orgasm went on and on, aided by the fact that Jeff refused to slow down and give her body a reprieve. He hammered into her until he was certain she could come no more. Only then did he slow his pace and eventually stropped thrusting altogether.

He slipped out of her and sat back on his haunches, wiping the sweat from his face and looking down at his glistening cock. He looked back at her hole. The lips gaped open, having been temporarily stretched by his thickness. He needed to keep fucking her and come himself, but time for a position change.

"On your back," he told her.

She slowly and rather stiffly got into position and opened her legs for him. As he entered her she looked into his eyes and smiled.

"I want you to squirt your cum all over my body."

"With pleasure."

Jeff set to work stroking her cunt and building up to his own climax. The three-quarter moon was providing plenty of silvery light now and he watched his cock disappearing into her pussy. Her lips wrapped tightly around it and were shiny with her love juice.

It took him no time at all to reach a climax and at the very last second he withdrew from her vagina and sprayed heavy wads of fresh cum all over her tits and stomach. One shot splashed off her chin and the last few dribbled onto the lips of her pussy. Kitty wiped the cum from her chin with the edge of her forefinger and licked it off. She smiled a sexually satisfied smile and sat up.

She said, "I think I need a swim."

* * *

It was Kitty's fourth night on the island and once more she was in Jeff's bed in his boutique apartment. She'd been there every night since their sexual encounter in the cove.

He got off her and dabbed sweat from his face with a tissue, then used the remote to crank the air conditioning up. His cock still throbbed and dribbled with both his cum and Kitty's juice. She sucked it clean for him, then went to the bathroom to freshen up. A few minutes later she returned and snuggled into his arms.

"I met a cute guy today while you were working," she confided openly.

"Oh yeah. Did you fuck him?"

"Not yet, but I want to. And he wants to."

"I thought *I* was your fuck buddy." Jeff was completely devoid of emotion regarding the other guy. He had no claims on Kitty. He enjoyed her company but, as with many before her, she was just sex.

"You are. That's why I want you to join us."

"I don't do gay," he assured her adamantly.

She giggled. "I'm sure Steve doesn't either, silly. I don't want you two to fuck each other. I want you both to fuck me."

Jeff contemplated it. He'd once had a threesome with a mate and his girlfriend, and that had worked out fine. There had been nothing remotely gay about it.

"I guess we could do that," he said finally.

She kissed his cheek. "Awesome. As a reward, I'm going to line us up a girl so you can have a three-way with two women. How's that sound?"

He nodded and grinned. "Awesome."

* * *

The next evening they went to Steve's holiday unit. He was vacationing with two mates, who were currently settled in at the bar downstairs to do some serious drinking. Apparently Steve planned to join them later, after he'd gotten his rocks off.

Kitty was trembling with excitement when she knocked on Steve's door. Jeff wasn't quite as excited. Not only was he not keen to share Kitty with another guy, he also didn't trust that the man might not be a closet guy, or bisexual. If this Steve guy tried to deliberately touch him at all, Jeff would be straight out the door. He'd voiced that to Kitty on the way over and once more she assured him that Steve was as straight as he was.

When they entered the apartment Steve and Jeff shook hands. The man was about the same age, height and build as Jeff and they immediately hit it off.

As the three drank a beer, Kitty asked Steve, "You sure your friends won't be coming back any time soon? Two men at once is enough. I don't think I could handle four."

Steve grinned. "They'll be drinking for hours. Trust me."

Kitty was wearing skimpy denim shorts and a white singlet with no bra. She stood up, ripped the singlet from her torso and shed her shorts. She wore no panties either. Steve's eyes roamed over her nakedness and Jeff saw him lick his lips in anticipation.

He said to Steve, "She's fucking hot, isn't she?"

"Damned straight." The other man got up and started stripping off. "I've gotta get into this."

Not wanting to be left behind, Jeff kicked off his boat shoes and slipped out of his shirt. He remained seated on the couch and eased his shorts and underwear down his thighs. His cock sprang to attention, letting him know it was in the mood for yet another good fucking.

Overcome with lust, Kitty was already on her knees on the carpet and greedily sucking Steve's long dick. She pumped four or five inches of his length into her mouth and had a handful of his heavy balls. Jeff got up and stood beside Kitty. Her left hand instinctively reached for his cock and she stroked it while she sucked Steve. After a few minutes her mouth wrapped eagerly around Jeff's member while Steve's was now wanked off with her right hand. She alternated like this for a good ten minutes, raising both mens' arousal to the verge of explosion. But she always knew just when to stop.

"I need a dick in my kitty and one in my mouth," she said and spread herself out on the lounge. "You guys can decide who fucks me first."

Jeff and Steve looked at each other.

"You go first," Jeff said unselfishly and straddled Kitty's face so she could take his wanton member deep down her throat. Behind him Steve knelt on the carpet and penetrated Kitty's cunt with his long staff. As his dick fed into her, Kitty swallowed Jeff's entire length. He felt himself throb down the back of her throat and had the overwhelming desire to come in her mouth tonight: something he'd yet to do. He sensed she might be agreeable to that, so he'd just do it when the time was right. "How's his cock feel?" he asked her when she took a break from sucking him and was busily lashing her tongue rapidly across his ball sack.

"Wonderful," she said. "Steve goes in really deep, and he knows how to use that beautiful cock of his."

As Kitty's mouth gorged his cock once more, Jeff said to Steve over his shoulder, "How's she feel, mate?"

"Fucking incredible! She's so fucking tight. She's gotta have the tightest, wettest little twat I've ever nailed."

"Give it to her," Jeff encouraged. "She loves it hard and deep. You'll make her come for sure."

Steve hammered Kitty's pussy while Jeff drove his throbbing meat down her throat. She couldn't seem to get enough of their cocks. He guessed having two guys was her ultimate sexual fantasy and she was lapping up every delectable second of the experience.

She pulled Jeff's cock out of her throat so she could scream in ecstasy as a shuddering climax gripped her and shook her to the core.

"Oh my God!" Kitty cried. "Fuck! Fuck!"

Jeff watched her tremble beneath him and it made him smile. This girl sure was highly sexed and loved a good dicking. It'd be his turn shortly and he couldn't wait to offer her another pounding with his cock that she loved so much. Last night, amidst the throes of passion, she once again said she'd be recommending him to her girlfriends. In fact, she went as far as to suggest she'd recommend this resort to them for their next holiday just so they could take advantage of his loving.

He looked forward to that. Pressure would be on. He'd have to live up to a reputation, but he didn't mind that.

Jeff took her doggy while Steve sat on the couch to rest and have his cock sucked. Jeff slid his length into Kitty's ready pussy and buried it in to the end of her throbbing and very horny tunnel. She was hot and wet inside, her pussy burning for more fucking action. And he was only too willing to give it some.

He watched her head bob up and down on Steve's rigid shaft as he slowly stroked her cunt from the rear. Right now he was content to just pleasure them both slowly with his tool; the plan to gradually build up the tempo and heighten her arousal before really going for it and giving Kitty another mind-blowing orgasm.

Steve rather lovingly stroked the young woman's dark hair as she gave him head. He had a permanent smile on his face. And why wouldn't he? Kitty was a blow job expert as well as a hot fuck.

Speaking of fucking, Jeff increased his pace, stroking Kitty's cunt with long and very deep strokes. He watched his cock plowing her passage and marveled at how much the thickness of his dick stretched her lips apart. He was turning himself on watching the action. It was like viewing porn and being a part of it at the same time.

He spanked her ass, first the right cheek and then the left. Jeff repeated the process a few times before gripping her hips once more and fucking her to an earth-shattering climax. She very nearly choked on Steve's dick, which was deep down her throat when the orgasm rocked her. She finished with a shiver and a loud moan, holding Steve's cock in her hand and stroking it slowly as the climax ebbed from her body. Jeff thrust into her slowly for a moment longer, then pulled out and sat back on the couch to relax. He truly thought Kitty's desires were spent for a while, but he was wrong.

She straddled him in the couch, facing him, and lowered her raunchy mound onto his shaft, burying it deep and moaning loudly toward the ceiling.

She turned to Steve. "I need a cock in my ass. I want to be impaled on two luscious dicks at once. Can you do that for me?"

Steve didn't need to be asked twice. He lubed up his cock with some spittle and, as Kitty leaned forward as far as she could, he knelt behind her and probed her anus with the head of his dick. His cock entered her suddenly, causing her to gasp in both pleasure and surprise.

Kitty did all the work, rocking back and forth on her two magnificent dicks, driving both in and out of her horny orifices with immaculate precision. Jeff determined she'd done this before, two guys at once, double penetration. She knew what she was doing and seemed very comfortable and confident with it.

"This feels so good," she whispered in Jeff's ear. "I can't tell you how good this feels right now."

"Probably as good as it's going to feel when I have two women," Jeff replied.

"Don't worry," said Kitty as she continued to slowly ride them. "I'll keep my promise and find us a girl to play with."

"Can't wait."

Jeff squeezed her melon boobs, felt the nipples stiffen into his palms. He wished he could suck on them, but in his current predicament there was no way that was possible. He could sense Kitty building toward another climax. She certainly knew how to come. No issues there.. Jeff could only imagine how intense this orgasm was going to be, with two cocks stimulating her passages.

"I'm in heaven," she swooned as the tension rose inside her. "My cunt is on fire, Jeff, and so is my ass." She took a very deep breath. "I'm...gonna...come."

A tremendous howl escaped from deep down her throat then. It rose in volume and pitch until Jeff thought the empty beer bottles on the nearby coffee table were going to explode. They didn't, but Kitty did.

She shuddered and trembled and moaned and groaned, all the while driving her cunt and ass down onto both Jeff's and Steve's cocks. Sweat ran in rivulets down her face, back and chest from her efforts. Juice flooded her cunt and formed a pool on Jeff's loins as she obviously squirted. He squeezed her tits for her to heighten the experience, twisted the nipples and felt even more juice eject from her out-of-control pussy. Her climax went on and on and lasted for well over a minute. When she was finally done, she slumped forward, not moving except for her chest heaving as she caught her breath.

Steve exited her ass and sat down on the floor. Jeff's cock was still buried deep within Kitty and he was in no hurry to remove it. Even without any thrusting, being inside her felt divine.

"You okay?" he asked her when she still hadn't moved.

"I'm fine," she said in barely a whisper. "That one really drained me. I'll be alright in a minute."

"I need to come," he told her.

"I'll make you come."

"I want to come in your mouth," he said, hoping she'd agree.

Her reply surprised him. "I want you both to come in my mouth."

Kitty had recovered enough a few minutes later to set to work bringing both Steve and Jeff to a much-needed climax. Once again Jeff unselfishly let Steve go first.

Steve sat on the couch while Kitty knelt on the floor and worked his cock in and out of her expert mouth with the help of her right hand. His balls were taken into her left, adding to Steve's stimulation. Steve closed his eyes and groaned as Kitty worked away on him with great enthusiasm. It took about three or four minutes for Steve to come. When he did he let out a series of satisfied grunts as he shot his load down her throat. Kitty smacked her lips with pleasure when he was done and crawled across the floor to position herself between Jeff's legs.

Jeff couldn't wait to come in her mouth. Something about a girl swallowing his cum really turned him on. It was like the greatest sexual compliment. He reclined on the lounge, half laying down on it, closed his eyes and waited for the warm, velvety feel of Kitty's mouth to engulf his member. She didn't make him wait. With his shaft gripped firmly in her hand, she wrapped those soft and moist lips around the head and took four inches of his length down her throat. Her tongue swirled around the head and licked at his shaft as she bobbed her head up and down and jerked his cock off with her hand. Fingernails of her other hand scratched lightly at his balls, sending tingles all through his body. Jeff sighed with immense pleasure and massaged her hair.

"Come down her throat," he heard Steve say. "She loves it."

Jeff concentrated on reaching a climax. He could tell by Kitty's actions that she was hungry for his cum.

"Suck the cum from my balls," Jeff urged her. "I want you to swallow every drop."

Kitty increased her tempo and sucked really hard on the head while wanking his dick furiously. Jeff felt the tension rise, his blood pressure boil over and the tingles of release form in his loins. The first shot of cum splashed deep down her throat. It was followed up by a succession of even bigger wads of man juice. She did indeed greedily consume every drop, and even squeezed more from his shaft when he was finished by running her thumb and index finger from base to tip.

No sooner had Jeff shot his load and Steve was hurriedly getting dressed so he could head downstairs and join his mates for a drink.

* * *

It was Kitty's last night on the island and, as promised, she'd managed to find a cute young female who was willing to join her and Jeff in a threesome.

The plan was to meet at the pool bar at seven. Jeff went down early and plunged into the resort pool, with its little bridges and artificial beach, to cool off from a very hot day. He'd worked all afternoon outdoors, showing new arrivals around the resort. Thankfully the temperature had cooled considerably with the setting of the sun, and a light sea breeze had wafted in around six.

Jeff had yet to set eyes on this girl. Apparently Kitty had met her today while snorkeling. Her name was Tatum. She was reported to be pretty, petite, with small, pert breasts and shortish blonde hair.

With all the sex he'd been having the past week or so, Jeff figured his desires should be somewhat satiated. But it was the opposite. Having Kitty around only served to fire his passion even more. And with the prospect of a threesome with another sexy female...Well, the mind boggled. He couldn't wait and found he had a constant hard-on while swimming lazy laps around the pool.

By the time seven o'clock ticked by the sun had set completely and a half moon should soon be rising over the eastern mountains. Jeff was tiring of indoor sex and planned to propose another outdoor session. Something he and Kitty hadn't done since their first scintillating encounter.

He'd dried off and had his towel wrapped around his waist when he spied Kitty walking hand in hand with a very petite blonde which could only be Tatum. To Jeff's surprise Tatum greeted him with a peck on the lips and a quick hug. Wasn't shy. That was good. Kitty greeted him in the same manner. While they indulged in a cocktail each, Jeff put forth his idea of doing it out in the open.

"I'm up for it," Kitty said with a nod.

"Sounds kind of romantic," Tatum said.

As romantic as a threesome can be, Jeff thought.

When they'd finished their drinks the three headed off in the direction of the headland and the private little cove. Jeff had a girl either side of him and the three walked arm in arm along the sand until they reached the rocks and had to venture inland on the trail. When they emerged in the cove, Tatum let out a soft whistle of appreciation and immediately undressed. Jeff thought she was keen to get right into fucking, but instead she sprinted into the water and dived in with a splash. Kitty and Jeff looked at one another, shrugged, removed their own clothing and joined Tatum in the sea.

The ocean was warm and invigorating. Even though the water was dark, Jeff didn't fear sharks as the outer reef kept any big and threatening ones at bay. He dived underwater and surfaced right behind Tatum, who was already engaged in a tongue kiss with Kitty. Jeff wrapped his arms around both girls and ground his stiffening manhood against Tatum's cute little ass. She immediately ditched Kitty, twisted round and thrust her wet tongue deep down his throat.

Jeff's cock throbbed against the hair above her snatch. He tongued her furiously and felt Kitty come up behind him and start playing with his butt cheeks.

Jeff needed to fuck these girls. A swim could come later. He broke the kiss and, without a word, grabbed each girl's hand and dragged them up onto the beach. They didn't bother drying off, just made a blanket on the sand utilizing Jeff's towel and all their clothing. Jeff then plonked himself down and indicated for the girls to go down on him. He wanted to experience two women sucking him off and sharing his dick. This was his ultimate sexual fantasy.

The girls complied eagerly with his wishes, just as keen to give him what he wanted as much as he wanted to receive it. They took up positions either side of him. Kitty held Jeff's fat cock upright and angled it towards Tatum's mouth, indicating she could have first taste. Tatum swallowed the tool rather greedily and sucked hard while Kitty pumped it in and out of Tatum's lips. Kitty then abruptly pulled the dick from Tatum's desperate mouth and engulfed it with her own.

Jeff was in ecstasy as he lay back on the ground and stared up at the sparkling stars. Having two women giving him head was the best sexual sensation he'd ever had. Kitty and Tatum swapped his cock between them constantly. While one intensely sucked him, the other would either wank his shaft or tongue-lash his balls.

Oh, what a feeling!

The blow job went on for at least ten minutes, maybe fifteen. Jeff wasn't complaining, but by now he was getting quite desperate for some pussy action and he voiced his desires.

"I want one of you on my face and the other on my cock."

With the two girls facing each other, Kitty sat on Jeff's open mouth and he immediately darted his keen tongue into her soaking wet cunt. Tatum, meanwhile, experienced the feel of Jeff's dick inside her for the very first time. When it entered her all the way, she sighed with satisfaction, relief and pleasure. Slowly she rose up and down his shaft, feeling every inch of his generous and rock-solid length.

"You weren't talking it up," she gasped to Kitty. "His cock feels truly amazing."

"I know," Kitty replied. "I'm going to recommend fucking Jeff to all of my single girlfriends."

Everyone fell silent then and got on with the business of fucking, licking and sucking. Kitty rocked back and forth on Jeff's face while Tatum kind of swirled around on the end of his dick. Every so often he heard the girls kissing rather wetly, at which time their actions all but ground to a halt. When they ceased kissing the riding and rocking would start up again.

Jeff lifted Kitty's ass off his face a few inches so he could speak and be heard. "I want you girls both to come. When you have, I then want you to swap places."

Both girls focused their attention on attaining a climax each. Tatum went to town on his cock, bouncing up and down with great vigor. Kitty reached a hand between her legs and strummed her clitoris while Jeff tongued her cunt lips furiously. He could sense the tension rising in both women. Kitty he already knew could come at the drop of a hat. He wasn't sure if Tatum was wired the same way.

In the end there was no need for him to be concerned when both girls managed to climax virtually in unison. Kitty came first, gushing hot juice all over Jeff's face and filling his mouth to overflowing. He swallowed as much as he could, not wanting to waste the precious fluid her pussy was offering him. Tatum started to erupt about ten seconds after Kitty exploded. The young girl screamed into the night and finished herself off with a dozen rather awkward thrusts onto Jeff's cock.

When they were both done they immediately switched positions and Jeff took great pleasure in biting into Tatum's juicy, peachy cunt for the very first time. Her lips were waxed smooth, but the strip of brown pubic hair above her clit tickled his chin. Kitty wasted no time sitting on his cock, and once she was firmly impaled she rode him hard and fast, obviously intent on bringing herself to another crescendo very quickly.

Tatum's delicious pussy tasted just as sweet as Kitty's kitty. She was extremely wet, smelt divine and an endless river of warm juice trickled into Jeff's mouth and down his thirsty throat. He sucked hard on her cunt, drawing those succulent soft lips into his mouth and reaching out with his tongue to lick her clit at the same time. Tatum loved this. She moaned and panted, reached around and roughly grabbed a chunk of his hair. She ground hard against his face as he sucked her furiously. Suddenly she quivered and squirmed, let out an almighty howl and squirted all over his face; which was still damp with Kitty juice.

He'd made her come in no time.

Tatum climbed off his face and Jeff sucked in some deep breaths of the warm night air. Kitty continued to pound his cock. The look on her face in the gloom was intense. She was getting close again, concentrating hard. Tatum got in behind her and continually spanked her ass as if spurring on a race horse. Kitty came then. Her strokes slowed as her muscles seized up. She let out a few gasps as the juice flowed forth from her passage, drowned Jeff's loins and formed a wet patch on his towel beneath.

The moment her climax had abated, Tatum reefed Jeff's cock out of Kitty's cunt and swallowed him right down to his balls. Jeff groaned with immense pleasure and felt like coming in her mouth there and then. He held back, however, and got his ejaculation urges under control. It wasn't time to come yet.

He took Tatum doggy while Kitty spread herself out on the ground and had her pussy licked enthusiastically by Tatum's ravenous mouth. Both girls panted and moaned as they were licked and fucked. Five minutes later and Jeff ordered them to swap around. Now Kitty was being drilled from the rear while she tenaciously ate out Tatum's juice patch.

It was a complete turn on watching these girls enjoy each other sexually. Jeff's arousal levels were at a peak tonight that he'd never reached before. Having two girls was just something else.

He nailed Tatum missionary next while Kitty rode her face. Jeff and Kitty tongued while they fucked and rode. He could taste Tatum's juice on her lips and tongue, and it made the kiss all the more sweeter. Once more they swapped around. As Jeff stroked Kitty, Tatum engulfed his mouth with hers and tongued him furiously. She licked his lips, sucked on his tongue and drove hers deep down his throat. It was an awesome kiss and these girls were a great fuck.

They both came again, first Kitty and then Tatum. The trio tongue kissed in a three-way, then Kitty pushed Jeff down onto the ground and the women set to work sharing his dick with their eager mouths once more.

Kitty grinned at Jeff while Tatum was busy sucking him. "We're going to make you come and we're going to share your jizz."

Jeff sure liked the sound of that!

He was so aroused that it took no time at all for the girls to make him climax. He shot squirt after squirt into the air for the girls to take turns catching in their open mouths. When he was done, Kitty and Tatum kissed deeply so they could share and savor his juice.

The three then ventured into the water for another swim, where they frolicked playfully under the light of the half moon.

Jeff floated on his back for a while and gazed up at the stars. It had been a fantastic past ten days and he couldn't wait to meet some of Kitty's girlfriends in the not too distant future.

Spice It Up

I returned to the table with the round of drinks. A bourbon and coke for myself, beer for Jake and vodka, lime and soda for Sara. Giving me the full body scan as I arranged the drinks on the table, Sara broke into a broad smile. As I sat down, she placed a warm hand on my forearm and looked me right in the eyes.

"So what do you think?" she asked, a twinkle of hope in her deep blue irises.

Jake and Sara were married and had been spicing up their sex life lately by including other partners. We'd all been in contact via an adult dating site for the past few weeks and tonight had decided to get together for drinks to see if we all clicked and felt comfortable. Jake was straight and so was I, so there was no question about anything awkward there. This was all about having two men to pleasure Sara. Indulging in group activity was something I'd never done, but was always curious to try. So when Jake and Sara contacted me, my interest piqued.

I nodded. "I'm happy to try it." I sipped some bourbon. "How about you two?"

Jake and Sara glanced at each other and communicated some unspoken message between them. Sara them focused her eyes on me again, nodded, then smiled. "We're definitely up for it." She took a large swallow from her glass of vodka. "I'm getting tingles now just thinking about it."

"Why don't you give Aden a small taste of what's to come," Jake said to her.

The entire time Sara hadn't taken her eyes off me. She moved in close, her eyes half closing as she did so, and locked her soft lips on mine. Next thing I knew my mouth was wide open and filled completely with her wet and hungry tongue. We kissed passionately for several exquisite minutes. When Sara broke the embrace my cock was as hard as a slab of granite inside my jeans.

Sara smiled lewdly. "How was that?"

"Can't wait for the main course," I replied while clearing my throat.

Jake downed his beer and got to his feet. His wife followed suit, finishing her vodka with a hurried gulp. I took a little more time polishing off my bourbon as I didn't like to drink fast. When I'd drained my glass I got up, feeling quite loose and relaxed from three bourbons and a shot of tequila.

Jake and Sara led the way in their car while I followed close behind in mine. Their waterfront home was only five minutes drive from the tavern. As they pulled into the driveway I pulled in behind them and trailed them into the house.

It was open plan with a kitchen looking out over the pool and canal outside. Being the middle of winter I figured were weren't going to play out there. Instead, Jake lit a fire in the fireplace to warm up the living room. There was a comfortable looking couch not far from the flames and, right in front of the fireplace was a plush red rug. An armchair sat opposite the couch on the other side of the fire. Jake and Sara took up positions on the couch while I slumped into the chair.

"So how's this work?" I asked naively.

Sara looked at her husband, who raised an eyebrow. "How do you mean?" he asked.

I shrugged. "You guys have done this before and I haven't. I guess I'm just trying to get my head around it all."

Sara responded. "Meaning, how does Jake enjoy seeing another man fuck his wife?"

"Yes."

"It's a turn on, Aden," Jake said easily. "I know this sort of thing's not for everyone, but we enjoy it. Sometimes a male joins us. Other times it's a woman. Sometimes another couple. Sara and I have a very strong but open relationship."

"And we only ever play together," Sara put in. "Never alone."

I looked at Jake. "So if I'm really enjoying fucking Sara, that's not going to bother you? You're not going to mind?"

"Hell, no!" Jake assured him. "The more everyone enjoys themselves the better it is." He turned to Sara. "Right, Honey?"

"Absolutely." Sara's eyes were on me, a faint smile curling the corner of her mouth. "Just relax and enjoy yourself. Play with me as if I was your own woman."

"If you feel a bit uncomfortable at first, mate," said Jake, "just sit back there and watch us for a while, and join in when you feel ready."

I nodded. "That sounds like a good idea."

So I did. After emptying my pockets, removing my shirt and

taking off my shoes, I settled back to watch the action unfold before me.

Jake and Sara started off by kissing heatedly and caressing each other through their clothing. Sara was wearing a black skirt, white blouse and black stockings. As her husband's hand roamed along her thigh, she parted her legs to expose not her underwear, but her lush naked pussy. Jake's finger probed the fleshy lips of her cunt, stimulating her clit, then thrusting inside her. She broke the kiss and let out a moan of delight. Reaching for the buttons of his shirt she quickly undid them.

As they got each other worked up, every now and then she glanced sideways at me, obviously enjoying my eyes on her as she prepared to get naked with her husband. My cock was throbbing with tremendous energy in my pants. The jeans were restricting my member, so I stood up and took them off, leaving me clad only in tight white boxer shorts. Jake and Sara were disrobing at the same time I removed my pants and I caught Sara's grin as she eyed the bulge in my underwear.

She realised I wasn't quite ready to join in yet when I sat back down in my chair, so she returned her attention to her now naked husband.

Jake stood there; tall, lean and muscular with his erect cock right in front of Sara's face as she sat naked on the couch. Sara was curvaceous with small and petite breasts. She sat with her legs spread wide apart so I had an unimpeded view of her luscious cunt while she set to work on Jake's cock. She stroked it with her left hand while caressing his shaven testicles with her right fingertips, all the while greedily sucking on the head of his shaft.

I found myself wishing that it was my cock she had in her mouth right now. But I didn't have to wish. She was there for the taking. All I had to do was strip off my underwear and make my way over to the couch.

And so I did.

Sara alternated between sucking her husband's cock and mine. Jake had a larger piece than me, but I didn't care. Sara seemed to be equally enjoying both.

As Jake watched his wife's mouth engulf my meat he said to me, "Are you enjoying that, mate?"

"God yeah!" I replied, not taking my eyes off Sara.

"Good." Jake knelt on the couch. Sara slid her mouth off my cock and positioned herself on the couch on her hands and knees. I watched as Jake directed his cock between Sara's pussy lips and slid easily all the way inside her. She gasped as he did so, enjoying the full lengths of his thrusts.

I slowly stroked my cock and just enjoyed watching the action for a few minutes. My attention was diverted when Sara patted the arm of the couch, signaling for me to sit there so she could work on my cock some more while being fucked doggy by her husband. I obeyed, positioning myself right in front of her wet and hungry mouth. She attacked my cock with venom, sliding the entire length down her throat in one slick and practiced motion. The intense sensation almost caused me to explode right then and there, but I managed to control myself and hold back my load.

Jake watched his wife suck my cock while I watched Jake fuck his wife. It was an interesting scenario to say the least.

Sara's tongue ran down my shaft and found my balls, where she licked and sucked for a while before returning her attention to my dripping dick. Jake was literally hammering her sodden cunt now and I saw Sara shudder as she came for the first time. Jake continued to thrust into her with long and powerful strokes until she reached a second climax. As her orgasm subsided, Jake pulled out of her and got up from the couch.

"Your turn, Aden," he said. "Fuck her and make her come again."

The positioning changed. Sara sat on the couch with her cute butt right near the edge and spread her legs for me. I knelt on the floor in front her, where she reached down and grabbed my cock in her hand. She guided me to her parted lips where I eagerly entered her.

The sensation of her tight wet flesh on my cock was incredible. She had a truly gorgeous pussy. The lips were completely shaved smooth with just a small plume of dark pubic hair above her clitoris. I watched as my cock went in and out of her dripping wet hole in a smooth rhythm. I took it slowly at first, closing my eyes and luxuriating in the feel of our hot flesh melding together. When I finally opened my eyes again, Jake's cock was deep down his wife's throat. Watching this heightened my excitement and I began to pound Sara's lush cunt more vigorously. I gripped her thighs and drove in deep and relentlessly. My increased tempo and fervor caused Sara to let Jake's meat slip out of her mouth so she could pant loudly and uncontrollably.

Jake looked at me, smiled and nodded approvingly. I was doing well.

I slipped out of Sara and stood up. She immediately descended on me and took my length into her mouth to taste her own juices. I let her do this for a minute or two, then pulled away from her. I was feeling very confident now and suggested we continue fucking in a different position.

Taking up a place on the couch I had Sara position herself on top of me but facing away from me. With one hand placed behind her on my chest, she guided my dick into her slit with her other hand and commenced riding me with expert thrusts.

Jake took a break for a while and sat in the chair, watching the action contentedly.

"Hope it's okay to say this, Jake," I said as I watched Sara's ass rise and fall before me. "But I absolutely love fucking your wife."

"Glad to hear it," came the reply. "Judging by the look of intense pleasure on her face right now, I'd say Sara loves fucking you too."

Her hand reached down and stroked my smooth balls, sending tingles all through me. Her pussy made a loud slurping sound as she rode up and down with the gentle motion of a wave. Juice dripped down my shaft and drenched my balls, where it cooled pleasurably. I gripped her hips and thrust into her from below. Our needy bodies slapped together, harder, faster, deeper. My hands searched out her petite and supple breasts. Her nipples were erect and I teased them between my fingers. Sara leaned forward them and rode my cock hard, driving it into her depths, hands placed on her thighs to steady herself. She was building herself up for a climax, I knew. Her breathing was shallow, her moaning more urgent. I could feel her cunt squeezing tighter around my shaft. Sara was about to explode.

Her third orgasm of the night was her most intense yet. Maybe it was the new cock inside her that heightened it? Or the fact that her husband sat there watching her get off on fucking another man senseless? Either way her howling told me the experience was nothing short of mind blowing. Eventually her climax ebbed and her thrusting slowed. She tilted her head around.

"Do you want me to make you cum?" she asked sweetly.

I nodded.

She slid off my raging cock and positioned herself on the couch beside me. Taking my dripping wet cock in her hand she commenced stroking it up and down, encouraging my swollen and aching balls to let loose their load.

Jake watched with interest from the chair, wanting his beautiful wife to make me squirt.

It didn't take long. I felt the tingling sensation increase with every stroke of her hand. Sara was milking me expertly. After several more pumps the first wad of hot cum exploded from the head of my cock in a jet. She kept stroking and I kept cumming until my chest and stomach were bathed in sticky fluid. Sara tasted me by running her tongue through the pool of cum, then sucked the remaining drops from my cock.

I took a break after that and watched Sara and Jake lick, suck and fuck for the next half an hour. Sara had her fourth orgasm of the night and Jake his first. He shot his load down his wife's throat as she finished him off with her mouth.

Still Sara was hungry for more. With her husband spent for the moment she turned her attention to me once more. By now I was more than ready for round two. I was eager for more sex and keen to cum again. She knelt in front of me and lovingly took my cock into her hands, caressing the sensitive head and rubbing my balls simultaneously. I could feel a sense of power and raw energy running through my prick. Pre cum was oozing from the tip. Sara wiped some off with a finger and tasted it. She smiled and tasted some more, then wrapped her horny lips around my dick and worked it in and out of her mouth. I closed my eyes, enjoying the sensual pleasure she was inflicting on my manhood.

"Fuck that feels good. You sure know how to suck a cock, Sara."

My words encouraged her to suck even harder. The sensation was so intense I almost had to ask her to stop. Not because I wasn't enjoying it. The pleasure was nearly too much too handle. Sara continued sucking greedily for several more minutes, then I took her by the armpits and brought her up on top of me so I could suck her breasts. I alternated between each one in turn, enjoying the nipples stiffening in my mouth. Her flesh was silky and soft, contrasting with the hard, rubbery nipples.

As I feasted on her chest, Sara edged her way up a little and straddled me. Next thing I felt her hand reach around and lift my cock into an upright position. She lowered herself onto it until my pulsing shaft fully penetrated her soaking cunt.

Her feminine flesh was hot and steamy, searing the skin of my shaft as her pussy marinated my meat with its succulent juices.

I bit into her neck as we fucked on the chair. My hands grabbed her ass and squeezed tight. I slapped her cheeks hard several times and she cried out in pleasure and pain.

"Do that again," she urged.

And I did, spanking her twice as hard this time. A moment later she climbed off of me and turned around. This time she guided my cock into her ass. It was extremely tight on entry but felt really good. She rode me gently for a while and stroked her husband's cock as he stood in front of her. When Jake was fully erect, she leaned back and spread her legs really wide. Jake immediately entered her and drove his big cock deep into her cunt.

Sara said, "I love a fuck sandwich. The only thing I'm missing now is a cock to fill my mouth.

"We might try and line that up for next time, Babe," Jake promised her as he hammered away at her pussy.

Jake's humping motion served to drive Sara's asshole up and down on my cock. She was screaming with euphoria now and I knew with two cocks in her she was going to have her most powerful and intense orgasm of the night. Jake was slamming into his wife. He wanted her to climax and so did I.

She didn't make us wait long. Another dozen thrusts from her husband and her body started to quiver. She squealed with delight as her flesh convulsed in orgasm.

I could feel the tension building in my own body. My balls tightened as they prepared to unleash their juice. Tingles surged through my loins and up the shaft of my cock as my cum was released, expelling my load deep in Sara's ass. No sooner had I finished when Jake grunted as he reached his own climax and filled Sara's cunt with him cum.

Jake rested against his sweating wife a moment, the firelight playing on all our naked figures. Then he slipped out of her and stood up. Sara slowly got off me, cum oozing from both her holes. She walked rather awkwardly over to the couch and lay down, her sexual needs satisfied and her body exhausted.

I stayed where I was in the chair, enjoying the afterglow of fantastic sex.

Jake had disappeared from the room. He returned with three beers. I accepted one gratefully, feeling suddenly thirsty. Jake handed Sara a beer and sat beside her on the couch. He then looked at me.

"So, Aden. Can we talk you into coming back for more next weekend?"

Sexpert 2: Virgin Newlyweds

Sexpert Mandy was spread-eagled on the couch. Sharon's hot, wet and shaven pussy was firmly planted on her mouth while Sharon's husband, Mick, pounded Mandy's pussy with his extensive dick.

They were nearing the end of a two hour training session. Mandy had already managed to orgasm twice and was hoping for a third before their time was up.

The inexperienced couple had done well. At first both of them had been really tentative, having lived rather sheltered sex lives and totally lacking in confidence. But after a few wines and loads of encouragement from Mandy, both Sharon and Mick had really loosened up in the last hour, started letting go of their inhibitions and were really enjoying themselves. And that was the key: Really enjoy what you're doing, do it with passion and confidence and ultimately you will do it well.

And Mick was certainly doing well right this minute. He was stroking her pussy beautifully with great rhythm, variations and deep penetration. Mandy's twat was on fire. Mick's dick was sending streams of tingles all through her and it felt wonderful. Being in the profession she was in it was very difficult to hold down a steady partner or relationship, and she plain didn't have the time to go out and try and pick up. Therefore, her job as a sex instructor also served to fulfill her sex life. She needed to be pleased just as much as anyone else, and the better her students were, the more sexually satisfied she was as a result. The other great thing about her job was that she almost always trained couples, which served to satisfy her other desire; to be with a woman. She was totally bisexual and needed the attention of both men *and* woman regularly. Having said that, she got plenty of sex. Mandy lived in a large city and her services were extremely popular. Many couples enjoyed the experience so much that they booked her again and again; not so much for the training on subsequent visits, but for the three way pleasure. As it was she was having sex at least seven to ten times a week, sometimes more; and often for several hours at a time.

Sharon's pussy was soaking wet with sweet juice and Mandy was drinking as much of her precious honey as she could manage. Her lips, tongue and chin were covered in it and she had Sharon moaning uncontrollably as she plunged her talented tongue in and out of the young woman's cunt.

Mike had Mandy's ankles in a vice-like grip as he continued to pound her relentlessly on the edge of the couch while kneeling on the floor. He was only early twenties, well-muscled and in his prime; and used his powerful physique to really give her lush channel a good flogging.

Mandy moaned into Sharon's pussy as Mike brought her to her third climax of the evening. Her pussy squirmed and quivered and her body shuddered as the waves of pure pleasure washed over her. She bit into Sharon's clitoris in her excitement, causing the woman to squeal in pain. Mandy kissed it better with her lips and tongue, then Sharon got off and sat beside her on the lounge so she could watch Mandy and her husband fuck.

"You need to cum, Babe," Sharon said to Mike.

He nodded, his focus on watching his long cock slide in and out of Mandy's burning cunt.

"Pull out and squirt your man juice all over my big tits," Mandy suggested with an authoritative tone.

"Huge tits," Sharon corrected and Mandy smiled as she also watched Mike thrust into her.

His swinging balls slapped into her ass cheeks with every stroke. They were heavy and full and seriously needed emptying. She looked up at his face, which was a picture of concentration. His eyes closed momentarily and he groaned. When they opened again he pulled his cock out of Mandy and stroked it in his hand, sending hot wads of thick, milky jiz all over Mandy's breasts and stomach. Mandy leaned forward and squeezed her boobs together to catch the last few squirts. When he was done, Mike inserted his spent cock into her cunt again for a few final thrusts, then pulled out and collapsed into an armchair.

Sharon was on her then, busily licking and sucking her husband's cum off Mandy's flesh before it went cold. Mandy shivered from the tickling sensation of her slippery tongue and played with Sharon's hair as she feasted.

"You two are very quick learners," Mandy praised them. "You both went from being afraid to do anything at first, to be seasoned whores in the end. Good stuff!"

As the sexpert got dressed in skimpy red underwear and slipped back into her customary red robe, Sharon stuffed an envelope full of cash into Mandy's handbag. She then exchanged an expectant glance with her husband.

Mike cleared his throat. "Can we book you again in a few weeks?"

Mandy gave the couple her warmest smile. "Of course. It would be a pleasure to teach you some more. Twenty percent discount for a follow up session."

"Wonderful," said Sharon.

"Probably won't be for about two or three weeks," Mike said.

"Just call a few days in advance when you are ready," said Mandy. "I always enjoy the second time, to see how my students are progressing."

Mike and Sharon, both sexually satisfied, content and with renewed confidence, walked Mandy to the door, where she disappeared into the night.

* * *

The sun was setting orange and red in the western sky as Mandy pulled her black BMW into the driveway of her waterfront home. She was dressed all in lycra and her dark hair was glued to her face in places with sweat. She was just returning from a vigorous workout at the gym and couldn't wait to go out back, strip off and dive into her beautiful pool.

After collecting the mail and entering the house, Mandy did just that, making a beeline for the back sliding glass doors and stepping out into the twilight. The outdoor lighting came on automatically when dusk set in and the entire courtyard and pool area were bathed in a soft and subtle yellow glow. The colours of sunset reflected off the smooth surface of the lake behind her home and she admired this as she climbed out of her body-hugging clothing and waded down the steps into the pool.

As the cool water rose up her naked and voluptuous frame, she luxuriated in the invigorating sensation it gave her. She loved her pool and couldn't think of ever living in a place without one. Mandy ducked her head underwater and swam down to the far end, past a blue underwater light, and resurfaced beside a small cascade made of natural stones. The water poured over the rocks and splashed in the pool with all the calming sounds of nature.

A three-quarter moon was already rising in the east and would soon be replacing the sunset colours with its silvery glow.

Mandy moved under the tiny waterfall and let the pressure of the water massage her scalp. Tonight she had no appointments and actually was looking forward to having the evening off. A part of her craved sex, but mostly she just felt like chilling out tonight. She'd had a quick one hour tutoring session that morning, which went very well, so she felt rather satisfied with the one orgasm for the day. Besides, she could always bring herself to climax later if she really needed to.

As she floated around the pool on her back, staring up at the sky, she tried to imagine being in some other line of work and couldn't. She had an extremely high sex drive, needed to make good steady money, and also had some class and style. What better profession to be in then, than a sex tutor. And she considered herself to not only be experienced, but very good at her job. How could you not be when you loved doing something so much? It was a passion of hers, not just a job.

By the time she got out of the pool it was fully dark and the moon had risen higher in the sky. Mandy padded her fine skin dry with a towel and enjoyed the feel of a light breeze against her bare flesh. Her nipples stiffened under its gentle caress. It felt really, really nice. From an outdoor table she picked up a pack of menthol cigarettes, extracted one and lit it with a silver lighter. Mandy didn't smoke much, only about four or five a day, but always enjoyed one after a refreshing swim in the evening. When she had time for a swim that was. She was halfway through it when her cell phone rang and vibrated away on the tabletop.

She picked it up and answered it. After working through the greetings and pleasantries, she said, "So how can I be of service to you, Simon?"

"My fiancé and I have our wedding this coming Sunday," Simon said. "It's a late afternoon wedding with the reception going until about nine in the evening. After that we have a honeymoon suite booked at the Condor Hotel, before flying out to Noumea on Monday for our honeymoon."

"Okay," Mandy contributed.

Simon went on. "We were wondering – and I know this is pretty short notice – but Carla and I were wondering if we could book your services for an hour and a half on Sunday night. At ten o'clock."

Mandy was already on her way inside, where she went to her desk and flipped open her appointment book. This coming Sunday she had a one hour appointment at seven in the evening.

"I can do that for you, Simon," she crooned.

Mandy could almost sense his relief over the phone. "That's great," he said with a huge sigh.

Mandy smiled, glad to please. "So I take it you two want to brush up on your lovemaking skills before the honeymoon?"

There was a moment's hesitation on the other end, then Simon said, "Actually, we need a bit more than that. We have no experience whatsoever...We're both virgins."

That last bombshell stunned Mandy. Not that she hadn't encountered the odd virgin in the past, but this was the first time that she'd be coaching two at the same time; and a couple that had obviously waited until marriage before becoming sexually active.

But wouldn't this be a bit of a paradox and a conflict on interests for them? Saving themselves for marriage and then having a threesome with a sexpert?

Mandy shrugged and said into the phone. "What's your room number, Simon?"

"One-zero-eight-A."

She wrote that down in her appointment book. "Okay. I will see you and your new wife on Sunday at ten PM. And congratulations!"

Simon said," Thank you so much." Then he hung up.

Mandy put the phone slowly back down on the table and unconsciously lit another smoke. It was strange, both being virgins, both saving themselves for marriage, then sharing that sacred experience with a woman whom they had never met. She shrugged again. It was their choice, and it certainly wasn't her place to judge or assume or try and deduce people's motives and reasoning.

"Two virgins," she said into the night and puffed on her smoke. Mandy smiled then and suddenly found herself really looking forward to the challenge.

* * *

The night was cloudy and threatened rain as Mandy stepped out of her car and walked across the landing area of the Condor Hotel. She wore a red jacket that came down to her thighs. Beneath the jacket she was completely naked. Red fishnet stockings hugged her legs and her red stiletto-heeled boots clopped on the pavement. As usual her face was beautifully made up and her dark hair lustrous and full of life.

Outside the foyer doors she buzzed room one-zero-eight-A on the intercom and waited.

A moment later a female voice answered, "Hello?"

"Hi. Is that Carla? It's Mandy."

There was a nervous giggle. "Come up to the tenth floor and go left. Our is the apartment at the end of the corridor." There was a buzzing sound from the intercom then and the sliding glass doors opened silently. Mandy clip-clopped across the foyer tiles and entered the open elevator. She pressed 10 on the keypad, the doors slid shut and the lift started to rise. It reached the designated level within a matter of seconds, the doors parted like legs spreading and Mandy stepped out onto white carpet. She went left as instructed and knocked on the door at the end of the hallway.

When Carla opened the door her youthful looks took Mandy by surprise. The girl couldn't be any older than nineteen, way younger than Mandy's late twenties. Not that it mattered.

Carla was small and petite with shoulder-length, light brown hair. She was wearing a trimmed down, figure-hugging version of her white wedding gown; obviously having removed the extraneous parts such as the train for the reception. The bride led Mandy into a spacious sunken living area where a man as equally youthful as his new bride stood waiting expectantly. Simon still had on a black suit, the white shirt underneath looking a little disheveled and his tie half undone. He was tall and somewhat slender with short, dark hair. They were an attractive looking couple in a wholesome sort of a way.

They made the customary introductions and Mandy gave each of them a kiss on the lips in turn.

"Would you like a drink?" Simon asked. "We have beer, white wine and scotch."

"Wine will be fine," said Mandy with her disarming smile.

Drinks were taken outside to a courtyard area that had a hot tub bubbling away in the centre of it. The courtyard was totally private and had an unobstructed view of the city skyline by night. They all sat at a table and sipped drinks while admiring the view. They'd only booked an hour and half of her time, but Mandy knew some people needed more time to ease into things. Especially two virgins.

"Mind if I smoke?" she asked them.

"Go right ahead," said Carla, blue eyes bright in her lightly tanned face.

Simon got up. "I'll get you an ashtray.

Mandy lit up and studied Carla a moment. "I've never instructed two virgins before."

Looking a touch embarrassed, Carla looked down at the ground and said, "Is that a problem?"

"God, no. It's just not very common these days." She blew smoke into the night, where it was whisked away by the breeze. So far the rain held off.

"I'll be honest with you," Carla began. "Simon and I only saved ourselves for marriage to satisfy our old-fashioned parents. Even though we're both virgins physically, psychologically we want to be wild and adventurous when it comes to sex; and that includes experimenting with multiple partners and satisfying my bisexual tendencies."

Mandy smoked quietly for a moment as the husband returned with an ashtray for her. Carla's last revelation had also taken her somewhat by surprise; partly with what she'd just said and partly because she was so blunt about it. Unusual for someone so inexperienced. This was going to be a lot of fun, Mandy knew. These two, wanting to instantly broaden their sexual horizons and expand their boundaries would do anything she asked them to, just to please. She ashed her cigarette and sipped her wine, tingles of excitement and anticipation coursing through her veins.

"I was just telling Mandy how we really want to be swingers and that I'm bisexual," Carla said to Simon.

"Excellent!" Simon said with obvious approval.

"So you guys have no experience whatsoever?" Mandy asked.

Simon shook his head and Carla said, "But we've watched plenty of porn, so we have some ideas."

"And we've played around a bit without going all the way," Simon added.

"So you have some foreplay experience then," said Mandy and took a long puff on her smoke. "Why don't you two show me how you kiss."

Simon cupped his wife's face gently in his hands and brought his lips into contact with hers. Their kiss was rather tentative at first, nervous that Mandy was scrutinizing perhaps, but then they both seemed to relax, mouths opened and tongues started to explore. The kiss became more heated and urgent, both of them now breathing rapidly as their excitement escalated.

"That looked good," said the sexpert as Simon and Carla broke the embrace. She leaned in close to Simon then and said, "Now kiss me."

As Simon's tongue entered her mouth, Mandy immediately felt her pussy dampen. He kissed okay for a relative beginner. She tried to encourage his tongue to move around inside her mouth a bit more by retracting her own tongue. When he didn't respond, she broke the kiss and said, "Use more tongue. Don't stick it right down my throat, but also don't be afraid to fill my mouth with it. Also, open your mouth a bit wider so both our tongues have access to each others' mouths."

Simon nodded obediently and they tried again, with great results. Mandy held the embrace for a good two minutes, thoroughly enjoying the pash. She then pulled away and leaned across the table so Carla's mouth could reach hers. The young woman was a natural-born tongue kisser and Mandy luxuriating in the sensual touch of another woman's mouth pleasuring hers.

Mandy sat back down in her seat, lit another smoke and sipped her wine.

"Why don't you two strip naked and get in that hot tub," she suggested. The newlyweds obeyed and Mandy took particular pleasure in perving on their naked flesh as it was exposed layer by layer. They entered the bubbling water and nestled in close together. "Practice your kissing and fondling and I'll be in shortly."

As they pashed, Simon cupped one of Carla's pert little breasts in his hand. Carla's hand roamed over his chest, then sank beneath the turbulent water and Mandy assumed she was eagerly stroking her husband's cock. Mandy continued to smoke and drink and watch, all the while her pussy was getting wetter and wetter. She was ready now to join them in the water and really get this show on the road.

Mandy stood up, slipped off her boots and her robe, then slowly rolled her stockings down each leg. These she placed on the table and moved over to the edge of the spa. The horny couple had stopped kissing now and were both ogling Mandy's curvy and very voluptuous naked body as she slipped into the water.

"You sure are smoking hot!" Carla said, her eyes wide.

"Awesome," Simon simply said.

I can live with 'smoking hot' and 'awesome', Mandy thought as she edged in close to the others.

They indulged in a three way kiss for a while, mouths open and tongues lashing everywhere. Now and then mouths would clamp down hard on one another for a deeper kiss, then they would swap so everyone got an equal turn.

"Have you licked Carla's pussy before, Simon?" the sex instructor asked.

"No," he said with a shake of his head. "We never took things that far."

"So you haven't sucked Simon's cock either then?" she addressed Carla, who shook her head also. Mandy patted the wooden platform surrounding the hot tub. "Put your cute little butt up here then, Carla, and I'll teach your loving husband how to perform the art of cunnilingus."

Carla got out of the water in record speed and sat on the edge as instructed. Without being told, she spread her legs wide, giving Mandy a great view of her semi-shaven cunt. The lips were smooth and the pubis covered in a thatch of thick, dark-brown hair. Mandy's mouth watered as she eyed Carla's virgin territory.

She got in close to Carla's snatch and breathed in her succulent aroma. Her slit was slick with both water and juice and Mandy could feel the heat coming from it.

She turned to Damien, who was moving in close himself, and said, "Just watch me for a minute, then you can have a go." Mandy grinned. "I bet you're just dying to taste your wife's pussy for the very first time.”

He nodded like an excited kid and Mandy brought her lips and tongue into contact with Carla’s cunt. The moment she did, Carla shivered and gasped in a high-pitched tone. Carla gasped again as Mandy’s hot, wet tongue flicked over her clitoris. Mandy licked, nibbled and sucked the swollen erogenous zone, at the same time working her middle finger inside Carla’s tunnel. She was soaking wet now. Mandy withdrew her finger and put it in Simon’s mouth. His eyes lit up when he tasted his wife’s sweet juice and he sucked greedily.

“God! I’m so turned on right now,” said Carla, leaning back on her hands with her eyes closed.

“So am I,” Simon said. “And I’m only just watching!”

Mandy devoured her hungrily then, sucking, licking and slurping at Carla’s drenched passage, occasionally flicking her tongue over her clit. Carla was panting heavily and squealing with pure delight as the sexpert pleasured her.

“Can Simon have a go now?” asked Carla, her eyes open again.

Mandy moved her face away, which was slick and shiny with juice. “Sure he can.” She got out of the way and Damien took up a position between the outstretched legs of his sexy wife.

The first few lashes of his tongue were a little tentative as he tried to pleasure Carla’s clit the way he’d seen Mandy do it. “Don’t be afraid of it,” Mandy told him. “The more you enjoy doing something, the more pleasurable it will be for your partner.”

Simon suddenly sucked his wife’s cunt into his mouth then and ate her like a starving man. Carla screamed as he inflicted intense sensations upon her. She reached a hand down between her legs and pushed his head hard against her and held it there so he could tongue her as deeply as he possibly could.

Feeling the urge for another kiss, Mandy sat up on the edge of the spa and snaked her needy tongue into Carla's open mouth. Their wet lips locked as Carla's own tongue slid down Mandy's throat. Mandy toyed with her firm titties as they kissed and Simon continued to energetically devour his wife's beautiful cunt. When she'd satiated her mouth to mouth urges, Mandy dropped back into the water, came up behind Simon and reached a groping hand between his legs, where she massaged his heavy sack before taking his bigger-than-average cock into her hand. It was quite thick and very hard, radiating heat of its own as she slowly stroked him up and down.

"I think it's time you learnt how to give head, Carla," Mandy crooned as a light, misty rain began to fall.

Without a word, husband and wife quickly switched places, leaving Simon sitting there with his waiting dick dangling out in front of him like a pleasure pole. Over-eager, Carla got between her man's legs and fumbled with his cock and balls. Mandy moved in and gently nudged Carla out of the way. Both women got up onto the step, one each side of Simon's legs.

"Just watch for a bit," said Mandy and then flicked her tongue over the throbbing head of Simon's virgin cock. As Carla had done when Mandy first touched her pussy, Simon shuddered and gasped with euphoria. She held his wet balls in her hand as she drove half of his length down her throat. Then she withdrew to the head and sucked it hard and vigorously. Stroking his shaft while she worked the head between her lips, Mandy breathed hard through her nose and almost smiled when the realization struck her that this was the very first mouth Simon's cock had ever been in. He was as hard as steel, pre cum leaking from the tip, and Mandy was really enjoying giving him head; so much so that she almost forgot she was supposed to give his wife a go. She let his dick fall out of her mouth and looked at Carla, whose eyes were wide with excitement. "You have a turn now." Carla took Simon's dick in her hand and brought her lips into contact with the shaft, where she licked up and down it for a while, then spent a few moments nibbling on his balls. "That's the way, girl. You're showing initiative. Now take it into your mouth." Carla did, gorging most of it down her throat on the very first attempt. Mandy clapped. "We've got a wild one here." She looked at Simon, whose eyes were half closed and his expression one of serious intensity. "I think she likes sucking your cock, Hon."

He smiled. "And I think I like her doing it."

Mandy didn't bother giving Carla any further instruction. She was a natural and Mandy just let her go for it. In the meantime she tongue kissed with Simon for a while before getting back down in the water and wrestling the dick from Carla so she could have another suck on it herself.

"Am I being greedy?" Carla asked with a grin.

"You're allowed to be," Simon answered as Mandy went to town on him. "You're my wife."

Wife and sexpert proceeded to take turns with Simon's cock. While one would suck the other would either lick the shaft or take his balls into her mouth. They pleasured him like this for a good fifteen minutes before finally Mandy put a stop to the oral, so they could move onto the all-important next phase: The art of fucking.

"Fuck!" Simon exclaimed, then repeated it, "Fuck!"

Mandy grinned. "Does that mean you enjoyed that experience?"

He nodded adamantly. "Fuck, yeah."

"Speaking of the word 'fuck', that's what we're all about to do."

Carla rubbed her hands together. "Yum. Can't wait. Do I get to go first?" she asked hopefully.

"I'd like you to watch *me* first." When she saw the look of disappointment on Carla's face, she added, "Just for a minute or two, then you can have a turn."

Carla nodded her agreement and Mandy straddled Simon while he lay back on the deck. She placed one hand on his chest and lifted his dick upright with the other. Bending right over so she could see between her legs, she was satisfied that Carla had come in close and had a good view as she lowered her pussy onto his tool. It slipped in easily. Mandy was drenched down there and her pussy was squirming inside, begging to be completely filled with hot meat. Using her body weight, she lowered herself all the way down Simon's lengthy shaft until he was consumed up to his balls.

As Carla watched with extreme interest, Mandy gave her tips on varying the lengths of the strokes, the tempo, different angles in the current position, massaging his sack while she rode him and anything else she could think of. To Simon she suggested he play with her huge breasts while she rode his cock.

Mandy's cunt was making slurping, sucking noises as she bounced up and down. She'd promised Carla a turn after a few minutes, but now that she had this much-needed dick inside her, she felt very reluctant to take it out. However, when she felt Carla's hand on her ass, Mandy slowly rose and let Simon's dick slip out of her. She dropped down into the spa as Carla positioned herself above her husband in a squat. Mandy placed a hand on Carla's butt and held Simon's staff upright and guided it into his wife's cunt for the first time in their lives.

Carla gasped and grunted loudly as she struggled to take it all the way inside her tight virgin pussy.

"Just take your time," Mandy said. "Relax yourself. Don't thrust until you feel totally comfortable with it inside you."

Eventually Carla managed to take every inch of her man in and she commenced slowly bouncing up and down. Her tempo gradually increased as she relaxed and grew in confidence. Mandy, meanwhile, contented herself with massaging Simon's sack and Carla continued to improve her technique under the sexpert's instruction.

"You're doing really well, Carla," she praised. "How's it feel, Simon, to be fucking your wife for the very first time?"

"Awesome," he said. "She's so damn tight."

I bet she is, thought Mandy. Way tighter than me, no doubt.

"I think it's time you worked on your technique now, Simon," the instructor suggested. "Hop off him, Carla, and swap positions with him." They did and Mandy straddled Carla as she lay prone on the deck and opened her legs wide as Simon got in between them. She leaned over and grabbed Simon's cock, helping to guide him into his wife. "Be gentle on her at first," said Mandy. "Wait until she's fully comfortable again before thrusting hard."

She felt a finger slip into her dripping cunt then as Carla toyed with the offering that was positioned only inches from her face. Mandy realized that Carla had not had the chance to taste another woman's pussy yet, so she lowered herself onto Carla's mouth and felt the young woman's tongue slither its way inside her.

The girl was as natural at cunnilingus as she was at giving head. The way she worked her lips and tongue was incredible. Carla was going to give many a man and woman tremendous pleasure over the coming years if the two did indeed indulge in the swinging lifestyle they planned to adopt.

Simon was doing well for his first time making love. He was stroking rhythmically into his wife with long, deep strokes and Carla was dealing with it very comfortably. His eyes were fixated on the sight of his cock disappearing into Carla's very wet cunt. As Carla's mouth continued to eat Mandy's pussy, the woman leaned forward and tongued Simon while he steadily fucked his wife faster and harder. Soon he was nailing her like a seasoned expert and Carla was moaning loudly as she took a breather from lashing Mandy's snatch.

"Keep that up," Mandy whispered in Simon's ear, "and you'll give your wife her very first orgasm."

That thought spurred Simon on to even greater things. Carla had really loosened up the longer they went. She was completely relaxed and her pussy was soaked with juice. Mandy sat beside her on the deck and massaged her boobs to add to the girl's stimulus. The older woman could tell by the expression on Carla's face and her body language that she was fast building to a crescendo.

As she came for the very first time, Carla screamed into the night sky and clutched Mandy's arm in a strong grip. The orgasm was intense and hit her like a train, leaving her exhausted and trembling in its wake. Mandy kissed the young woman gently and tenderly as she gradually calmed and slowly recovered.

"That...was incredible," Carla whispered, out of breath.

"How does it feel to give your wife her first climax?" Mandy asked the husband.

"Wicked," he quipped, an excited gleam in his eyes.

"You got any energy left in the tank to fuck me some more?" the sexpert asked hopefully.

He grinned and eyed her horny body with complete lust. "Definitely. Can I give it to you doggy style?"

"You're getting adventurous very quickly. It's great to see."

Mandy knelt on the ledge that ran around the spa a foot below the bubbling surface. She waited expectantly while Simon got in behind her and felt the head of his cock nudge its way between the lips of her cunt.

The misty rain felt somewhat titillating on her bare back and Simon thrust his cock powerfully and confidently all the way inside her.

"Give it to her, Babe," Carla urged her husband. "Give the slut a good pounding."

"Slut?" Mandy said.

Carla kissed Mandy on the lips. "Sorry. I didn't mean that in a bad way. I'm just getting carried away."

"It's...okay," Mandy gasped as Simon drove his cock in an out of her. "It's healthy...to talk...dirty." After that she said nothing more, just panted and moaned and groaned as Simon continued to please her pussy. She was surprised at how good his technique was.

Carla was catching onto the threesome thing pretty quickly. She sat down on the ground in front of Mandy's face so the sexpert could easily lick her pussy. Mandy obliged and flicked her tongue rapidly over the younger woman's clitoris, causing her to squeal and squirm. Simon's cock ravaged her cunt as Mandy sucked Carla's snatch into her mouth and plunged her tongue deep inside her soaking tunnel. The added stimulation of devouring a fresh young pussy helped bring Mandy to a mind-blowing orgasm. She pulled her face away so she could scream as the climax took hold and shook her body like an earthquake. As the tremors continued, Simon didn't let up in his pounding. Mandy was still crying out in orgasmic bliss when Carla grabbed her by the hair and jammed her face back into her steaming pussy.

A moment later she had a second climax, not as powerful as the first, but equally as exciting. Finally, after the waves subsided, Simon pulled out of her so they both could rest a moment. Mandy collapsed into the warm water and let the light rain play on her face.

She watched as Carla took her husband's cock into her mouth again and practiced her newfound techniques. She sucked it and stroked it, tongued his sack and deep-throated him almost all of the way. A few minutes later and she was climbing back on for another ride. She squatted on top of him, facing towards Mandy in the spa, and rode him faster and faster until she was a blur of motion. Carla had Simon breathing hard and gasping with pleasure and Mandy thought he might be about to cum.

Carla beat him too it, her tempo slowing dramatically as her body convulsed in climax and she screamed into the night.

When she was done, Mandy and Carla shared Simon's cock, as they took turns licking it and sucking it, getting him hornier by the minute and building his sexual tension. After showing Carla a good technique of how to milk it with her hand, Mandy left her to it so she could enjoy the experience of making her man explode.

And explode he did, shooting hot jiz high in the air. Some of it landed on his stomach, while some propelled into the hot tub, where it was rapidly consumed by the turbulence. Simon grunted loudly with every expulsion, his face contorted in a mix of pleasure and tension. By the time he was done, Carla's hand was drooling with cum.

"Taste some of it," Mandy suggested, and Carla did, licking the juices from his shaft and head.

She grinned. "It's an unusual flavor, but I don't mind it."

They still had twenty minutes of time left and Simon recovered very quickly. Mandy showed the pair a few more positions and ended up reaching another climax while she sat on Carla's face. The young woman came at the same time on her husband's dick, and just before their time was up, Simon grunted as he exploded again, this time deep inside his wife.

As Mandy rode the elevator down to the ground floor, once again she was overcome with an extreme sense of satisfaction for having just helped others improve their sex lives.

The Hard Bar

anny Andrews owned and operated a trendy, upmarket bar in the center of town called *Liquid.* He loved his bar and enjoyed his work. He had a passion for it. Not so much the alcohol and mixing drinks, but the social, fun aspect of it.

And he was perpetually single. Which was advantageous as his bar was certainly a draw card for hot women.

His manager, Carla, and bartender, Jamie, already had the bar open by the time Danny arrived. It had just gone dark so the hour was still early, and so far there were only a handful of customers seated at the tables or on the stylish lounges that lined one wall. One man in his forties sat alone on a stool outside, sipping casually on a beer and smoking a thin cigar.

Some lounge music, set to a low volume, was currently playing through the sound system. Later in the evening a DJ would be remixing some of the latest dance tracks from Europe. It wasn't really a venue where people danced - there was no dance floor - but his clientele had a penchant for those sorts of tunes. It was never played loud, though. His bar was a place where people came to chill, have some drinks, chat and have a few laughs. Those who really wanted to strut their stuff usually went to a night club.

Carla was busy arranging tables and generally making certain everything looked neat and symmetrical; which was her way. She had shortish black hair and an athletic little figure. Her fiancé often came to *Liquid* on weekend nights to chillax with some friends and spend some time with her, as she rarely had a weekend night off.

Tonight was Sunday, which meant it wouldn't be as busy as the previous two nights, but the place still managed to draw a decent crowd, even on week nights.

Behind the stylish bar with its colorful array of alcohol bottles and shimmering glassware, Jamie was busy concocting a couple of Mojitos.

"I'll take these out," Danny said to him. "Which table?"

Jamie smiled. "Those two hot babes on the lounge over there."

Danny turned and followed Jamie's line of sight. His eyes came to rest on two leggy brunette's. Both were wearing expensive-looking dresses which exhibited a lot of cleavage and had slits up the side to reveal some thigh. One of the women had almond-shaped eyes and looked to be part Asian.

He turned back to Jamie and grinned. "Looks like I timed this nicely." He picked up the Mojitos and carried them over to the table, greeting the ladies with a friendly smile and bright hello. "I'm Danny, the owner," he announced to them. "These first drinks are on the house."

"Why, thank you," said the one who looked part Asian. She offered him a smile with perfect white teeth. "My name is Melody, and this is my friend, Claudette."

Danny shook hands with the ladies and sat down for a moment to make light chit chat. It turned out the girls were in town on a holiday and tonight was their first night. Danny definitely sensed some strong, positive vibes emanating from both women, but especially Melody. She appeared to be the most outgoing of the pair. Tourist girls were the best to hit on. As they were only in town for a short time, there could be no confusion about what was expected.

By now the place was starting to fill up and the DJ was setting up in preparation for his session. Jamie and Carla were a little over-run at the bar, so Danny left the two ladies to their drinks and went to help out.

As the music cranked up the drinks flowed and the happy vibe about the place intensified. Danny was busy mixing drinks and making up trays of shots. There were plenty of gorgeous women in the place tonight, but he still had his eyes on Melody and Claudette. Melody, especially, kept making regular eye contact with him.

Carla was busy waiting tables, so Danny picked up the tray of shots and took it outside, where a large group of patrons were talking rather loudly and animatedly. As he stepped back inside, Melody got his attention and waved him over.

"What time do you finish tonight?" she asked him.

"Anytime, really," he said above the music. "But I won't be going anywhere while it's this busy."

"We're staying upstairs," said Melody. Danny's bar was located below a hotel. "We're going to go back to our apartment now to just chill out. Come and buzz our intercom when you're done. Apartment 1602." Both women gave him a look full of promise and he felt his hormones stir.

"Okay. I'll do that, but it probably won't be for a couple more hours."

Claudette said, "That's fine. We'll still be awake."

"And waiting," Melody said, lightly touching his arm.

The women left *Liquid* then and made their way to the hotel's foyer, leaving Danny wondering about the prospect of a threesome. He had to forget about that for now and concentrate on keeping *all* of his customers happy.

"Sounds like you're in with both of them," Jamie said a while later when they got a bit of a break behind the bar. Danny had just told him about the girls wanting him to come up to their place when he finished up. "You can get going if you want. Carla and I should be able to handle it from here."

Danny shook his head. "No rush. I'll stick around for a bit longer." He wasn't too sure why he was turning down Jamie's offer, but the bar was his, and his responsibility. Another half an hour or so wouldn't hurt him.

He poured himself a shot of tequila and knocked it back, loving the way it seared his throat on the way down. He contemplated having another, but decided to leave it. He would take a bottle of something upstairs with him.

By eleven thirty things had wound right down and the bar was now only a third full. Danny went out back and washed up, then took two nice bottles of red wine from the rack, said goodnight to Carla and Jamie and went round to the hotel lobby. Melody buzzed him up straight away and he rode the elevator to the sixteenth floor. When he stepped out into the hallway, he spotted her down the end holding the door to their apartment open for him.

"Hi," she greeted him, that gorgeous smile splitting her face.

Danny entered the spacious apartment, with its huge glass windows and ocean views, and placed the wine on the kitchen bench. The place was decorated predominantly in white and looked very modern and somewhat chic. Claudette was seated on a white leather L-shaped lounge. She smiled at Danny and gave him an extended look. Melody produced three wine glasses and Danny got to work filling them. The drinks were taken into the living room, where Danny found himself seated between the ladies. They all clinked glasses and drank up.

"This is a really nice apartment," he said, glancing all about.

Claudette said, "We like it."

"The bedroom's nice and roomy, too," said Melody, "with a king-sized bed."

"Really?" said Danny and he raised an eyebrow as Melody gave him a curious look. "I'll have to check it out."

"You will," Claudette said.

"We'll show it to you soon," Melody assured him.

We'll? Danny thought. That sounded very promising.

He got up and walked out onto the balcony, where he sniffed the sea breeze and gazed out over the dark ocean. Even up this high the sound of the waves rolling into shore was very distinct. He was aware of a presence behind him and saw Melody approaching. She stood close to him, so close the sides of their bodies were touching. He could feel her warmth and it was nice. Melody sipped her drink with one hand and placed the other on his back, gently massaging it through his shirt.

"You're very good looking," she said.

He grinned. "Thank you. And you are smoking hot."

She had a cheeky look in her pale green eyes. "Do you think Claudette is hot, too?"

He nodded. "Definitely."

"Have you ever been with two women at the same time before, Danny?"

Now they were getting down to it.

"A couple of times." And it was true. He had experienced a few male, female, female threesomes, all courtesy of meeting at his bar.

"So you're experienced then." melody stated. "We like a man who knows what he's doing."

"Are you offering me a threesome?" Danny got to the point.

Melody nodded, took him by the hand and led him back inside. Claudette had disappeared from the lounge and Danny couldn't see her anywhere.

"She's already in bed," Melody said, reading his thoughts. "She'll be naked by now and laying there waiting for us."

Those words instantly sent Danny's cock from flaccid to full hardness in the space of a few seconds.

"Then we'd better not keep the lady waiting," he said and Melody took him through to the very roomy bedroom.

Claudette was indeed lying naked on the bed, her figure exquisite and the light tan of her skin looking lovely in the lamplight. Danny's eyes roamed over her nakedness. The woman's breasts were round and plentiful, hips beautifully curved and her pussy was completely waxed smooth.

Melody dropped his hand and immediately stepped out of her dress. Her underwear was quickly removed and she joined her friend on the bed. Her body was almost identical to Claudette's; same size, shape and assets. She, too, kept her vagina hair-free.

"Get naked and join us," Claudette said.

"Yes, Danny," said Melody. "We're waiting."

With all eyes on him, Danny first kicked off his shoes and removed his socks. These were placed neatly near the wall. He slipped off his shirt, exposing his fit and tanned physique. The look of approval in the eyes of Claudette and Melody didn't go unnoticed. They eyed him expectantly, waiting for him to drop his pants and reveal his most vital asset. Danny gave them what they desired, shedding his trousers and underwear in the one motion. He stood there naked, cock standing proudly at attention, his balls hanging nicely in their shaven sack. Both women licked their lips as they checked out his erection.

Melody patted the bed. "Come here, lover."

Danny climbed onto the bed and instantly hands were roaming all over his bare skin. The girls refrained from touching him down there for the moment, content to feel the ridges of his muscles and the firmness of his behind. Their combined attention was sending shivers of excitement rippling through his flesh and he couldn't wait to really get into it.

Taking the lead, he lay down and got comfortable with his head propped up on two pillows. The ladies knew exactly what he wanted them to do and got into position either side of his hips. Lips were licked again as they prepared to taste his long and very thick cock. Melody touched it first, standing it upright so she could admire its size.

"You're quite big," she said.

"Over eight inches," he reported happily.

Claudette said, "So you've measured it then?"

"I think all men have measured themselves at one point," Danny admitted.

Claudette sampled his balls with her tongue while Melody wrapped her luscious red lips around the head of his throbbing member. As she sucked, Claudette licked, running her tongue up and down his length. The girls swapped then and Claudette had a turn gorging his member while Melody kissed his shaft and sack. Hands were all over his thighs and stomach and Danny just lay there groaning with pleasure. He loved his work and he loved his life. What a fantastic way to finish off a busy evening.

Both Claudette and melody were panting and moaning while they gave him head. Obviously the oral was increasing their own arousal, and it certainly was having that affect on Danny. He couldn't wait to feel himself inside their luscious wet pussies.

"Suck it," he said and the girls rapidly kept swapping his cock between their hungry mouths. He could see their lipstick coloring his shaft and that served to turn him on as well.

Melody took him deep down her throat while Claudette pushed on the back of her head. The woman choked when she reached the sin inch mark and had to withdraw. It was Claudette's turn next while Melody pushed her head. Claudette almost succeeded in swallowing him whole, but came up about an inch short. Not to be outdone by her friend, Melody had another go and swallowed him all the way down to his balls.

While Melody continued to enjoy his dick, Claudette kissed her way up his torso until her lips were on his. Danny thrust his tongue into her mouth and she did the same. What a feeling, kissing one hot babe while another kissed his cock. Claudette was good with her tongue and kissed just the way he liked.

While he tongued Claudette, Danny felt Melody's mouth move away from his cock. Judging by the movement of the bed she was climbing on top of him and preparing to mount him. He tongued Claudette feverishly the moment the head of his cock punctured the opening to Melody's extremely wet cunt. She moved up and down his length with fluid grace and already she was moaning.

Claudette ceased with the kissing, got up, spun around and sat on his face. Immediately his thirsty tongue sank into her depths. Her pussy was that wet it was like an ocean of juice inside her tunnel. And she was sizzling hot. Danny took great delight in tonguing her passage and swallowing her sweet essence. Her aroma was mouth-watering.

Melody was now slamming her cunt down onto his cock, her

pussy comfortably accommodating his dimensions. She was squealing now, a sound that became muffled when her friend leaned forward and kissed her.

Danny smiled into Claudette's muff. So these two were lovers as well as friends.

The sound of their kissing gave him the motivation to start thrusting into Melody. She met his strokes, slamming that wet little pussy don't onto him over and over again. And then it happened. Both girls reached a climax at exactly the same moment. Danny plunged his tongue into Claudette as she wriggled around on his face and Melody screamed as her body shook on top of him.

After resting for just a minute or two, the girls swapped. Melody's cunt was just as delicious as her friend's had been, and when Claudette sank all the way down his shaft, he marveled at just how tight she was inside. She rode him steadily and Danny kissed, licked and sucked on Melody's muff. The girl rocked back and forth on his face, stimulating herself all over. His hands had hold of her thighs as he strained to burrow his eager tongue as deep inside her cunt as he could manage. He felt Claudette hop off his cock and impale herself reverse cowgirl now. She leaned back into Melody's arms and bucked her hips, driving his shaft into herself at an unusual angle.

The girls didn't climax again in these positions, but all three loved the tryst nonetheless.

Danny pushed Melody off his face so he could breathe. Sensing a position change, Claudette bounced off his cock and lay flat on the bed.

"I wanna do you from behind," he said to Melody, "while you go down on your girlfriend. I assume you like eating pussy?"

"Very much so," Melody was adamant.

He let her get ready and waited until she'd made a start on devouring Claudette before he got in behind her and entered her once more. Danny watched as her pussy swallowed up his entire cock. He held it deep inside her for a moment, then started slowly stroking her succulent passage.

Melody was quite noisy as she went down on her friend. Not only was she making rather loud wet, sucking sounds, in between she was moaning and groaning from the pleasure Danny's cock was giving her. He increased his pace, thudding his body against her ass and making her scream.

"Take it," he said, his teeth clenched. He held her by one hip and placed his other hand on the mattress, thrusting faster and faster until she came all over his cock. By now she had stopped feeding on Claudette and just focused on negotiating her way through the euphoric throes and sensations of her orgasm. "That's it," Danny said. "Keep coming."

He collapsed on the bed when she was done, the muscles of his thighs starting to seize up. Gasping for breath, he watched as the girls moved around until Claudette was going down on Melody. She had her ass pointed skyward, hoping for Danny to do her doggie now. He gave himself another minute or two break, then entered her from the rear.

She groaned with immense satisfaction as his cock bullied its way to the end of her soaking tunnel and Melody giggled.

"That tickles," she said to Claudette, who was still moaning, the lips of her mouth jammed up hard against the lips of Melody's cunt.

Filled with renewed energy, Danny fucked Claudette hard and fast and deep. He constantly watched his dick disappearing inside her. Her lips were stretched wide apart to wrap around his very thick girth and he was proud of the size of his manhood.

"Make her come," Melody told him.

Five minutes - and many quick-fire strokes - later and Claudette came for the second time. Her orgasm was prolonged by Danny's incessant pounding of his cock into her pussy and she eventually fell forward to put an end to her pleasant torture.

The three took a break for a while and went to the kitchen to pour some wine. They took their drinks out onto the balcony where a breeze served to cool down Danny's hot flesh. He'd been working up a bit of a sweat and it felt good to take a few minutes RnR.

When they'd finished their wines they made their way into the living room, desiring a change of location for the next round.

Melody mounted Danny while he sat on the leather. Claudette was down on the floor, where she intermittently would wrench his cock from Melody's pussy and suck the juices off it. The girls changed places after five minutes and Melody did the same thing.

Danny then fucked Melody missionary while Claudette rode her face. It only took Melody a few minutes to make her friend climax on her mouth and Danny watched the other girl shudder as the waves of tension and pleasure swept through her. He targeted Melody for another orgasm and gave her one not long after Claudette's had subsided.

"I really need to come," he announced and sat down on the lounge. He looked at Melody, who was still his favorite. "Use your hand on me. I want you girls to watch it come out."

They both appeared to like that idea and Melody went to work stroking his big cock while Claudette hovered close by, watching and waiting expectantly. Melody was great with her hand and he soon felt the tingles form down below as his cock prepared to unleash its heavy load.

He came in powerful jets, shooting his cum high into the air before it splashed all over his torso. Both women were smiling as they watched the spectacle, then hungry mouths were all over him, lapping up his warm juice.

Danny felt really relaxed now and he closed his eyes as the ladies fed from his flesh.

Life didn't get any better than this.

Lesbian Lust

Tracey and Adele were live-in lesbian lovers, and had been in a relationship for the past three years. Both were in their late twenties, and were fit and attractive women.

The white satin sheets felt sexy against her naked skin as Tracey lay in bed waiting for her partner to come out of the bathroom. From a drawer in the bedside table she removed a six inch vibrator with clitoral stimulator. They'd only just bought it and tonight would be the very first time they'd used it. She briefly turned it on to check that the batteries had plenty of power, then placed it on the bed beside her. The only light in the room emanated from a small lamp with a red shade. The bedroom was cast in a soft glow of crimson and looked very romantic.

Adele finally emerged from the bathroom, her silky brown hair freshly brushed and straightened. She had on no make up and didn't normally wear make up to bed. She was completely nude, her shapely figure looking very inviting in the red glow of the bedroom. Adele slipped beneath the covers and Tracey took her lover into her arms. The pair kissed very lightly on the lips as hands started to explore one another's bodies. Tracey ran her right hand up Adele's smooth thigh, then cupped a cheek of her butt as Adele's wet tongue slid into her mouth. Tracey tongued her back and soon the kiss had evolved from soft and tender, to fierce and passionate.

Their collective breaths came in short, excited bursts as their arousal rapidly escalated. Tracey raked her nails down Adele's back as Adele took one of Tracey's soft breasts into the palm of her hand. Tracey felt her nipple stiffen under her touch and tingles of excitement rippled through her body.

The kiss went on and on. Tracey's pussy was flooded with warm juice and it was throbbing. She so needed to be touched down there, caressed and fingered and tasted.. Feeling impatient, she seized Adele's hand and placed it on her crotch as she opened her legs. Adele ran a finger up and down her wet lips before plunging it inside her tunnel. A second digit worked its way inside her and Tracey broke the kiss so she could let out a long moan of satisfaction. Adele now thrust those fingers into her faster and faster, making Tracey gasp and pant. Her lover used her thumb to stimulate Tracey's clitoris at the same time, and what a feeling it was, having her tunnel penetrated and her clit rubbed all at once.

"Kiss me," Tracey said and the two clamped mouths tightly onto one another once more.

Tracey sucked hard on Adele's tongue, eager to extract the juices from it. Adele then returned the favor and sucked on Tracey's tongue. Tracey's hand now searched out her lover's pot of honey and she was pleased to find that Adele was just as soaked down below as she was. Tracey slid three fingers inside her partner and thrust vigorously. Now it was Adele's turn to end the kiss so she could groan in ecstasy.

"My...God!" she exclaimed, eyes wide open and staring toward the ceiling.

Both women were now plunging their fingers rapidly in and out of each other's cunts. Lips came together once more and tongues thrashed heatedly and very wetly.

"I need you to go down on me," Tracey said hoarsely.

"And I need you to go down on me," said Adele.

They both smiled at one another then, knew what they had to do and got into a sixty-niner position. Tracey lay flat on the bed, parted her legs very wide apart and let Adele climb on top. When Adele lowered her pussy onto Tracey's face, Tracey immediately slid her tongue into her musky wet tunnel and probed as deeply as she could.

Adele was busily lashing Tracey's clit. She nibbled on the aroused nub, then ran her tongue down to Tracey's tunnel and plunged inside, tasting her deeply. Tracey sucked on Adele's entire pussy, while at the same time still sliding her tongue in and out of her warm passage. Both women kept their vagina's shaven smooth all over. A hairless pussy was much more pleasant to devour.

Tracey had both cheeks of Adele's firm ass in her hands and she squeezed them hard. Adele's mouth all over her cunt was driving her wild with desire and she couldn't help but squirm around beneath her. Her lover was building her up to a climax already and she could not wait to come on her face. Her pussy was absolutely throbbing now and she could feel tension building all through her body. It wouldn't be long now.

"I'm gonna come," she announced and Adele lashed her pussy with even more enthusiasm.

Tracey screamed as the waves of orgasm washed over her like

heavy ocean swells. She writhed around on the bed as her lover continued to pleasure her most erogenous zone. Tracey dug her nails into the flesh of Adele's hips as the tension came and went. She finished with a gasp, then lay still. Adele moved her face away from Tracey's pussy and gave her a moment to recover. Tracey just lay there sucking in deep breaths. Adele's pussy was still right in front of her face and it looked glorious.

She probed Adele's entrance with a finger, bringing a gasp from her friend. She was so wet. Searching the bed for the vibrator, Tracey switched it on and ran the throbbing head up and down Adele's slit, teasing her. She then placed the vibrating knob on Adele's clitoris and rubbed hard. Adele flinched with sensitivity, but didn't move away. Tracey moved it slowly down to her passage and worked several inches of it inside. Still teasing, she gradually pushed it in deeper until her pussy had swallowed the entire length. The clit stimulator was now firmly up against Adele's clitoris and her body started to quiver as the sex toy did its wondrous job of inflicting great pleasure.

"Fuck that feels good," Adele said. "It's so intense. Fuck me with it, Babe."

Tracey had one hand on the small of Adele's back as she rapidly worked the rubbery tool in and out of her sexy lover. Adele was so wet that her pussy made delectable sucking noises as it was fucked by the vibrator. The clitoral stimulator was doing a great job and had Adele quivering and shuddering.

"I'm going to explode in a second," Adele said. "Here it comes."

She let out a howl of delight that was so loud Tracey was sure the entire neighborhood would have heard it. She kept on plunging that vibrating rod into Adele's squirming, quivering pussy, extracting every ounce of pleasure from the climax, wanting Adele to be in a state of euphoria for as long as possible.

Adele pushed forward and the vibrator slipped out of her. "I can't take it anymore," she explained, gasping for air. "It was too intense."

"But good," said Tracey.

"Definitely good. Just hard to handle."

"Do it to me now."

Adele took the sex toy from Tracey and sat between Tracey's outstretched legs. There she teased Tracey's pussy like Tracey had done to her. The vibrations sent tingles all through her pelvic region. Adele was smiling as she played and grinned broadly when she aggressively thrust the artificial cock deep into Tracey's cunt, causing her to squeal in delight.

Tracey couldn't believe how good it felt to have that throbbing member deep inside her, pleasuring every inch of her tunnel while rubbing against her clitoris at the same time. Her brain was swimming with desire and she felt light-headed. She sucked in a deep breath, closed her eyes and concentrated all her focus on what was happening down below.

"Give it to me," she whispered to her lover.

Adele responded and fucked Tracey harder and faster with the tool, plunging it into her pussy with relentless vigor.

Already Tracey could feel another climax rapidly building. This one was going to be far more intense than the first and, like Adele, she wondered if she was going to be able to handle it.

It hit her like a volcano erupting. She felt it first down in her loins as he pussy throbbed with raw energy. It burst like a dam and intense waves of pleasure rippled through every nerve in her body. Juice gushed from her pussy as she squirted for one of the rare times in her adult life.

"Oh my God!" Adele said with a huge, satisfied grin. "Look at that. That's so awesome."

Just when she thought the climax was subsiding, Adele would roughly plunge that vibrator into her again, causing another wave to build and break. Again fluid jettisoned from her aching pussy and sprayed onto the bed.

"Pull it out," Tracey said desperately.

But Adele refused to obey. She fucked Tracey hard with the tool until Tracey was writhing around on the bed like a snake. She suddenly rolled away, fell off the side of the bed and collapsed in a heap on the floor. She was struggling to get her breath back and her pussy still throbbed like it had a life of its own.

Adele's face appeared over the side of the bed. "Are you okay down there?" She grinned. "It's intense, hey?"

Tracey managed to nod, but said nothing. Her breath was raspy in her constricted throat.

"Did you not like that?" Adele quizzed.

"No, I liked it...It was just a little too much."

Adele assisted Tracey back onto the bed, where the couple lay curled up in each other's arms for a long while.

"I don't think I can take any more tonight," Tracey admitted. "I know we weren't doing it for long, and I loved it, but I've had enough for tonight."

"That's okay, Babe," Adele said. "Maybe next time we won't use the toy."

"Maybe we just have to get used to it?"

"You might be right."

They both fell silent for a while, and Tracey was just starting to doze when Adele spoke again. Tracey's eyes snapped open at the sound of her lover's voice.

"What do you think about this idea?" Adele began. "We haven't been gay all our lives. We've both had men in the past, and we both enjoyed having men in the past."

"What are you getting at?" Tracey wanted to know.

"I'm thinking we should get a male into the mix. You know, not all the time. Just occasionally."

"Have a threesome?"

"Yeah, a threesome. What do you think?"

"I don't know. I must admit I do like cock and I miss it. Would you get jealous seeing a man fucking me?"

"I don't think so. Not if we were sharing the experience. Would you?"

Tracey thought about it. "I can't answer that," she said honestly. "I'd like to think I'd be okay with it. I wouldn't really know for sure until I was confronted with that situation."

"That's a fair enough answer," said Adele. "How about we try it once, and if it's really not for us, we'll never do it again. What do you say?"

Again Tracey pondered the suggestion. "I'm open to the idea, but where are we going to find a man?"

Adele giggled. "I don't think that task is going to prove to be a difficult one. What hot blooded male isn't going to want to have a three way with two hotties like us? The hard part will be finding the right man; one we're both happy to indulge with."

"The internet," Tracey said.

"Like a dating site?"

"An adult dating site. We see ads for them all the time on late night TV," Tracey said. "We put up a profile and state exactly what it is we're looking for. Guys get in touch and we screen out the ones we're not interested in and respond to those we are." She rolled onto her back and grinned. "You know, this could actually be quite fun; the process of finding a guy, I mean."

"And the end result," Adele added emphatically. "Let's make a start on this tomorrow night."

* * *

All day at work the next day Tracey kept finding her mind wandering. The more she thought about including a hot man in their lovemaking, the more excited she was getting. It had been a while since she'd been with a man sexually and, although she was happy and content in her relationship with Adele, she did miss a man's touch at times, and a man's body.

Finally five o'clock came and she headed home to find Adele already there cooking up a stir fry in the kitchen. They kissed a quick greeting, then Tracey poured two glasses of red wine and placed one on the counter beside her girlfriend.

"That smells yum," Tracey said.

"Hope it tastes as good as it smells."

"I'm sure it will."

When dinner was ready and served the pair sat down at the four-seater table to eat. The wine bottle was placed in the centre of the table so they could top up their glasses.

"Any idea what site we should put a profile on?" Adele asked Tracey as they ate.

Tracey shrugged. "No. We'll just do a search and see what we come up with."

"We'll need to take some sexy photos."

Tracey grinned. "Well, that should be fun. Have a shower with me after dinner. Then we'll get all dolled up and do some photography."

"I like the sound of that," said Adele and she started eating more quickly.

When dinner was done and everything had been cleaned up, they topped up their glasses and went into the bedroom, where they both undressed and got into the shower. Adele set the water nice and warm and it came out in a powerful jet. They took turns soaping up each other's bodies using a loofah and shower get, giving each other a soft and gentle massage in the process. As Adele rinsed the soap from

Tracey's skin, her free hand went between Tracey's legs and she started to rub her clitoris. Tracey closed her eyes and sighed. She desired to have just one orgasm; a climax that was not too intense.

"Finger me," she whispered. "I'm already wet."

While Tracey leaned back against the tiled wall and parted her legs, Adele got down on her haunches and thrust two fingers inside Tracey's hot, wet cunt. Tracey sighed a huge sigh of delight and could already feel the tension building. It wasn't going to take very long at all for her lover to bring her to orgasm.

Tracey grasped one of the tap handles as the climax rippled through her. She'd gotten what she wanted; a nice pleasurable orgasm that wasn't too intense.

The pair kissed now, tongues eager and rampant, mouths wet with water and desire. Tracey probed Adele's pussy with her fingers as they tongued, and when she slid two digits inside Adele's slippery passage, Adele pulled her face away and gasped.

"Lean up against the wall," Tracey instructed her.

When Adele was in position with her legs apart, Tracey knelt down on the tiles and ran her tongue all over Adele's pussy. She put her lips to her opening and sucked warm juice from her passage. Adele clawed at Tracey's hair, seizing clumps of it and pulling on it quite hard as her desire mounted.

"Fuck that feels good," she seethed through clenched teeth.

Now Tracey plunged her tongue inside as far as she could reach. Still Adele tugged at her hair and started grinding up against Tracey's face. Tracey thrust her tongue in and out in a rapid-fire motion, then proceeded to lash Adele's engorged clitoris. She nibbled it, sucked it, bit into it, then rang rings around it with her tongue.

As she pleasured her partner's clit, Tracey thrust several fingers inside her to stimulate her passage. Adele gasped and moaned as the shower water continued to cascade down onto the girls and the tiles.

"Give it to me," Adele swooned. "Make me come, Baby."

Tracey continued on with exactly what she was doing; fingering her cunt and lashing her clit simultaneously until Adele exploded on her face. Her lover shuddered against the wall a few times and bucked hard against Tracey's face as the climax released the pent up sexual tension from her body. Adele shuddered a couple more times, then was still. Tracey moved her face away and put her head under the stream of warm water.

When they were out of the shower and dried off, the women spent the next hour drying and straightening their hair and applying some light make up. Back in the bedroom they laid an array of sexy lingerie and underwear out on the bed. Tracey first dressed in some white knickers and matching bra while Adele slipped into a red and black camisole. Out in the living room they used a small compact digital camera to snap off some pictures as they adopted sexy poses on the couch. In the bedroom again they changed outfits, then took some more photos in the living room. On the third occasion, with the bed now cleared of clothing, they took up seductive poses on the bed for the camera lens to capture.

"Should we do some nude shots?" Adele wondered.

"I don't know," said Tracey. "What do you think?"

"Let's just do some topless shots," Adele decided. "Keep the rest a mystery."

They did one topless shot each, then went into the kitchen, poured more wine and took up seats at the desktop computer, which was located in a corner near the TV. Tracey first uploaded the images from the camera's memory card, did some light editing in a photo manipulation program, and reduced the size of the files so they would upload quicker to whatever website they chose to post themselves on.

She opened up Google and conducted a search for adult dating sites. Quite a few came up. After researching the first couple on the list they decided those sites weren't for them, but something about the third one appealed, so they decided to put up a profile. After creating a profile name, they input some details about themselves, then went into a little bit of detail about exactly what they wanted, and what type of guy would suit them. The next step was to upload the photos. They were allowed a maximum of ten. They only had eight, so there was no problem there.

"Done," Tracey said triumphantly. "Now I guess we sit back and wait for some hot guys to get in touch."

"Why wait when we can search for some right now?" Adele pointed out. "Come on. Let's do a search."

Tracey clicked on the search button and they input some details into the search criteria. Definitely preferring someone local, they limited it to a fifteen mile search radius. Tracey clicked the search now button and a list of possible candidates came up.

"Yuck. I don't like the look of that first guy," said Adele. She pointed at the screen. "Click on that one." Tracey did and the man's profile came up. "He looks alright. What do you think, Babe?"

Tracey clicked onto the guy's images. He had a very handsome and chiseled kind of face with deep blue eyes and a strong jawline. Another shot showed him wearing jeans and no shirt. The muscles of his torso were nicely defined. He wasn't too big, more of an athletic build.

"Yeah, I definitely fancy him," Adele said. "Send him a flirt."

Which was what it was called on this site; a way of expressing interest in someone.

"He's online now," said Adele, "so I hope he sends us a message tonight."

They spent the next half an hour drinking more wine and searching out more possible suitors. All in all they sent flirts to six guys. Now it was time to sit back and see who responded, and what they had to say. Ultimately they only wanted to meet one man to play with, so, depending on how many responses they got, they would then have to decide which guy was going to be the lucky one.

The computer speakers made a beeping noise.

Adele said, "What was that?"

"I'm not sure," Tracey admitted. She saw that a yellow number one had appeared towards the top of the screen over 'messages'. She said excitedly, "Someone's gotten back to us already." She clicked on the messages button and they both saw that there was a brief note from the very first guy they'd sent a flirt to.

Adele leaned in close to Tracey to read what it said. "I don't know," she said finally. "There's something I don't like about him. Sounds too up himself."

"I agree," Tracey said. She got up and went into the kitchen, where she opened a fresh bottle of red wine. So far she was getting a nice comfortable warm buzz from the alcohol and she was keen to add to it. "Anyone else messaged us yet?"

"Not yet," Adele replied, a tinge of impatience in her voice.

"Have some more wine," Tracey said, handing her a glass. "It'll make you feel better."

"Thanks." Adele took a long sip, draining half the glass before putting it down on the desk. "That's better."

"Another message has just come through," Tracey noticed as she took her seat. Hurriedly she clicked on it. It was from the very last guy they'd contacted. His name was Michael. He wrote a little more about himself and he sounded far less egotistical and more eager to please than the first one.

"I like the sound of him," Adele voiced Tracey's thoughts. "Let's write back to him."

"What do we say?" Tracey wanted to know.

"Just tell him we want to meet him," said Adele. "This coming Friday night. We'll meet him down the local for a casual drink. Then, if we're all happy with things, we'll bring him back here and have our way with him. Just write something like that."

"What?" Tracey said with a grin. "Have our way with him?"

"Well, don't write that exactly. Come on, get to it, girl. You're good at writing. Let's arrange a meet and greet, with the possibility of more."

"Friday's only two days away," Tracey pointed out.

"So? We want to do this, don't we? I say the sooner the better."

Tracey typed up a brief message and sent it. Within five minutes there was a reply. Again Tracey responded, giving a time and a place to meet on Friday night. Michael responded right away and said he would definitely see them there.

"Deal done," Adele said with a happy clap of her hands.

"Provided we fancy him when we meet him in person."

"I'm pretty sure we will."

* * *

For both Adele and Tracey Friday night couldn't come quick enough. As they had a bite to eat, showered and dressed in readiness to meet Michael, their arousal was growing by the minute.

"I'm actually wet down there right now," Tracey conceded as she slipped into a sleek black dress that barely covered the cheeks of her firm ass.

"I know what you mean, Babe," Adele agreed. "I'm feeling super horny tonight and can't wait to get going. I do think we'll like this guy. I just have a good feeling about it."

"I hope you're right, because I'll be feeling pretty disappointed and let down if nothing eventuates tonight."

They drove the short distance to their local bar, parked out back and went inside. Michael was already there, and was seated at a table in a corner near the bar. He recognized them right away and got to his feet to greet them. There were kisses on the cheek all round, then

Michael went to the bar and bought drinks.

"He's even better looking in person," Tracey whispered to Adele.

Adele said, "He's hot."

"And seems nice, too."

Michael returned to the table and placed glasses of champagne in front of the ladies and had a beer for himself. His alert green eyes repeatedly glanced at each of the girls and he seemed to have a permanent smile on that handsome face of his.

The three chatted lightly over their drinks and all got on well. He was very personable and likeable and Adele and Tracey kept exchanging glances of approval. By the time they'd finished a second drink the girls were raring to go and told their suitor so.

As they drove back Michael followed in his own car and parked it in the driveway of their home. Inside the house some wine was poured into three glasses and the trio relaxed in the living room. Michael sat in the middle of the couch with the girls flanking him.

"Where do you want to do it?" Adele asked and looked at Tracey.

"Right here," Tracey was emphatic, feeling a little tipsy by now. "I like doing it on the couch."

Everyone laughed at that and put their glasses down on a nearby coffee table. Adele moved quickly and already she had her hand on Michael's crotch. Tracey just looked on as the pair engaged in a very passionate and very moist tongue kiss. Adele rubbed Michael's stiffening member through the material of his trousers and Tracey could see the bulge growing very quickly. She wanted some of that, so she brushed her friend's hand away and took his thick cock in a firm grasp. Michael turned his head towards her and Tracey kissed him deeply, immediately feeling her pussy throb with desire and flood with juice.

Adele pulled Tracey's hand away from Michael's throbbing cock and went to work undoing his pants. "Have you ever had a threesome before, Michael?" she asked as she searched inside his underwear for his member.

He stopped kissing Tracey so he could answer. "Once, a few years ago."

Adele was now leaning on the floor and removing Michael's shoes so she could take his pants off. "Did you enjoy it?"

"I loved every second of it," he readily admitted.

Adele freed him of his pants and Tracey spent a moment admiring that long, thick cock that her girlfriend had now exposed. The skin of the large head was taut and shiny and she felt herself salivate. It had been quite a while since she'd had one of those in her mouth and she was keen as hell to suck it.

Adele beat her to it and wrapped her hungry lips around it, driving inches of it down her throat with the aid of her pumping hand. Tracey got down on the floor and moved her face in close. She flicked her tongue over Michael's smooth balls. He manicured himself down there and the skin was silky to the touch. His balls were loose and hung heavily in their sack. She greedily sucked one into her mouth as Adele continued to gorge is cock deep down her throat.

"Give me a turn," Tracey said and wrestled the dick from her friend.

As she took it into her mouth for the very first time, Michael was busy getting free of his shirt. He tossed it away onto the floor and was now completely nude. Tracey looked up at his face as she pleasured his tool. The look in his eyes was one of pure lust and sexual contentment. He smiled as he gazed down at her and gasped when Tracey sucked really hard on the head of his lush cock. It throbbed as she let it slide slowly down her throat. Next thing she knew Adele was wrenching it back off her so she could suck on it some more.

Tracey got to her feet, dropped her dress to the floor and quickly extracted herself from her underwear. Feeling even more sexy now that she was naked, she climbed onto the lounge and kissed Michael again so he could enjoy that pleasurable sensation while his cock was being worked on. His hands toyed with Tracey's breasts as she thrust her tongue down his throat, and she gasped when he wandered lower and ran a finger over her wet pussy. She willed that finger to venture inside her tunnel and Michael didn't disappoint.

She could no longer keep kissing him. She had to pant and pant hard as he now worked two fingers in and out of her cunt in a rapid movement. Adele was still intent on swallowing his large cock and she continually made loud, sucking and slurping noises as she did so.

"I want you to eat my pussy," Tracey said to Michael.

They altered positions. Michael lay prone on the couch and Adele resumed her oral. Tracey straddled Michael's face and lowered her steaming mound onto his parted lips. Immediately his tongue darted into her hole. Tracey leaned forward as tingles of pleasure swept through her pussy and licked Michael's hard shaft as Adele sucked tenaciously on the head. She gave Tracey a turn and she took the cock into her mouth as Michael fed hungrily on her extremely wet pussy. Adele sucked on his balls as Tracey took his length down her throat. It was so thick it stretched her lips to their limit to accommodate its girth.

Both of their tongues were now sliding up and down either side of his long shaft. When they reached the head on occasion the girls would kiss, tonguing each other with the cock between their lips. Tracey lightly scratched Michael's sack and could feel his testicles swirling around inside as if they were excited about the prospect of an ejaculation sometime soon. Adele's mouth ventured down there again and once more Tracey took Michael's length deep down her throat.

Adele got up and said to Michael, "I think you should fuck her while I watch."

Feeling desperate for male penetration, Tracey leaped off him so he could get up. She wanted to be taken from behind, so she knelt on the lounge with her arms on the backrest and pushed her ass out and up, inviting him to fuck her doggy. Michael got in behind her and nudged the head of his cock between her lips. Adele nestled herself into Michael's back and pushed against him, forcing his cock deep into Tracey's pussy.

"You feel so damned big," Tracey moaned. "God, that feels good. Fuck me."

Michael stroked into her methodically with long, deep strokes that massaged every bit of her internally. His balls slapped against her clit with each stroke, adding to the pleasure of it all. His big cock felt so beautiful and she'd so missed the sensation of having a man buried deep inside her. He'd only been giving it to her for a few minutes when Adele grabbed hold of his cock, pulled it from Tracey's cunt and wrapped her mouth around it, tasting her girlfriend's juices. She only sucked it for a moment, then inserted it between Tracey's lips once more and Michael continued on from where he was interrupted.

Tracey closed her eyes and gripped the padded backrest tightly. His cock was really doing the trick and she could feel herself slowly escalating towards her first climax of the evening.

"Make her come," Adele urged Michael. "Make her come all over your big dick."

She reached behind Michael and fondled his balls as Tracey started to scream on the couch. She felt tingles all over and her pussy throbbed as it erupted on this beautiful cock. Michael drove himself in harder, intensifying her climax and prolonging it. Tracey sucked in a deep breath as another wave burst within, then it had passed and she started to relax.

Michael withdrew from Tracey then and sat himself down on the couch. Adele got on the floor and gave him head while Tracey slumped in the corner to recover. There she watched as her woman sucked on a man's cock. Before tonight she'd never witnessed that before. She didn't feel jealous at all. They were sharing this special experience together and they were both enjoying themselves. In fact, she realised that she quite relished sharing a man with her lesbian lover. They should do this kind of thing more often. After all, they both still loved cock. Why not have a hot man in the mix once in a while?

Tracey joined her lover on the floor then and they took turns tasting Michael's rock hard member.

"I think you should ride it," Tracey said to Adele. "I wanna see his big cock inside you."

Adele looked at her and grinned lasciviously. "Okay. You feed it into me."

Tracey nodded and watched at Adele straddled Michael facing away from him, preparing to ride him reverse cowgirl. As she squatted down Tracey lifted his cock and held it in an upright position as Adele lowered herself onto it. Tracey watched from close up as Adele's wet pussy swallowed the entire length inch by succulent inch.

"That looks so beautiful," Tracey commented as Adele ever so slowly rose up his length until only the tip remained wedged between her soft and slippery lips. "Fuck it. Ride him hard and make yourself climax on it." To Michael, she said, "How's her pussy feel?"

"It feels incredible," he replied. "Nice and tight and really fucking wet. Just the way I like it."

"Come on, Babe," Tracey urged. "Ride him faster, or I'm pulling that cock out and sitting on it myself."

"Don't you dare," Adele said firmly and increased the tempo of her thrusting.

Michael had her by the hips and thrust into her from beneath. He did it in short bursts that pounded her in a flurry of strokes. Every time he did this Adele would stop moving and just take it, panting hard as he fucked her vigorously. Tracey couldn't resist. She needed to do two things at once; taste Adele and suck Michael's dick, so she pulled it out of Adele's passage and thrust it deep down her throat. Slowly her lips rose up the long shank as she extracted Adele's sweet juices from the taut, bumpy skin. Tracey then spent a few moments sucking hard on the head, causing Michael to groan loudly. When she was done she jammed it back into Adele's tight pussy, sat back on her haunches and watched the sex show once more.

"I'm gonna explode," Adele announced after only a few more minutes of fucking. She bounced up and down, faster and faster. Michael started slapping her ass as if egging her on, wanting her to climax all over his love wand.

"Come on it," Tracey barked. "I wanna see you come on it."

Adele literally screamed the house down when the tension suddenly released its vice-like grip. She was a blur of motion as she thrashed around on top of Michaels' member. He continued to slap her backside as she came all over him. Tracey saw juice trickle from her cunt and splash down onto his balls. She couldn't help but lick it off them.

"My turn for some reverse cowgirl," Tracey said and quickly switched places with Adele, literally pushing her out of the way so she could claim the pleasure bar. She wasted no time impaling herself on its rigid length and took great delight in swallowing it whole with her own tight twat. "Fuck this cock feels good. Why have we waited so long to do this?"

"Beats me, Babe," Adele said while watching Tracey ride Michael with extreme interest. "But we'll definitely be doing it again."

Tracey felt like she was going to come already. It had been so long since she'd had a man that her hormones were working overtime. There was definitely lots of sexual chemistry with this guy and he had the most wonderful cock imaginable. She couldn't remember a cock feeling so good, even in the days when she was full-on into men.

Adele put her head between their legs and tongue-lashed Michael's balls and shaft as Tracey rode him. Every time she rose up his length, Adele's tongue was there to sample the sheen of juice her pussy left behind. When she dropped, Adele would thrash his sack. This went on for a few minutes until Tracey pushed her female lover away so she could hump Michael faster and bring herself to another climax. She slammed herself down on Michael's member, driving it deep into her depths and making her rabid pussy squirm. Juice flooded her passage and seeped onto Michael's balls. Adele's eyes were open wide, as if waiting for something dramatic to happen.

And it did. When Tracey climaxed, fluid shot from her cunt and sprayed onto the floor. For the second time in a few days she was squirting, and God it felt amazing!

"Wow, Babe," Adele said with a huge grin. "That was awesome." She grabbed some nearby tissues and dabbed all around Tracey's pussy and Michael's package, then the floor beneath.

Tracey hopped off his cock then and took it into her mouth, where she sucked him hard and fast and plunged his member deep down her throat. Adele joined in, once more running her tongue up and down his length before having a turn swallowing it herself. Michael squirmed around on the couch, groaning as his cock was pleasured by two hot and sexy women.

Adele was taken missionary by Michael next while Tracey sat on her face. Tracey watched as that big angry cock plunged relentlessly into her girlfriend's sodden pussy. The visual increased her own arousal and in no time she came on Adele's face. There was no squirting this time, just a nice subtle orgasm.

They switched them and Adele got on Tracey's face while Michael penetrated her on the couch. He went in deep, ground the head of his cock into the very end of her tunnel, then slowly withdrew. His balls slapped against her ass every time he thrust into her and his cock spread her horny wet lips wide apart. Adele's cunt was very juicy and Tracey took great delight in sucking the honey from it. Sweet nectar coated her tongue and trickled down her throat. Adele had the best pussy and Tracey loved devouring it.

"Fuck her hard," Adele said to Michael in between soft moans.

Michael responded and upped his tempo until he was driving that cock into Tracey like it was his last night on Earth. Tracey couldn't help but moan and squeal into Adele's pussy as her male lover gave her the fucking of a lifetime. She could feel the entire couch rocking back and forth from the vigorous momentum and she knew she would come again any minute now.

As it turned out she came on Michael's cock just as Adele experienced a small climax on her face.

Adele was taken from the rear next and Tracey spread herself out on the couch so Adele could go down on her at the same time as she was being penetrated. Her tongue worked away enthusiastically, alternating between probing her wet passage and stimulating her clitoris. But as Michael started to fuck her harder, Adele was too busy panting and moaning to perform cunnilingus any longer.

After Adele climaxed once more, Michael positioned both girls on the edge of the couch and took turns fucking each of them. Every time Michael was thrusting into her Tracey was in heaven, but when he pulled out so he could pleasure Adele's waiting pussy, Tracey's felt empty and she couldn't wait for it to be her turn again.

He gave both women another orgasm, then he sat back on the couch to rest.

"Let's make him come now," Tracey suggested.

The girls worked away on Michael's cock while he sat there and relaxed. He had his eyes closed and was concentrating on reaching a much-needed conclusion. Tracey licked the head of his dick while Adele pumped it in her fist. In no time at all Michael's body tensed up and he started to groan louder and louder.

Cum shot from his cock in powerful bursts which soared high in the air and splashed onto his chest and stomach until there was a milky, viscous pool of it. When he was finished he let out a long sigh of relief, opened his eyes and grinned.

"I so needed that," he said.

"Didn't we all," both Tracey and Adele said at the same time and laughed.

Open Relationship

Her pussy was so wet and the way she was riding his cock threatened to make him come prematurely. Kyle forced himself to think about something non-sexual for a moment until that urge to ejaculate was under control.

Amy gasped repeatedly as she stroked up and down his shaft, plunging it deep inside her passage with every downward thrust. She sure knew how to ride him and once again Kyle fought to keep his urges of release under control.

He closed his eyes, took a deep breath and reached up to latch onto her bouncing boobs. They were plump and firm and easily more than a handful. The nipples were stiff and aroused and he felt his girlfriend shiver under his touch. Her pussy was so soft and wet and warm around his cock and every time she dropped all the way down he felt the head of his dick rub the end of her tunnel. Juice trickled onto his balls where it cooled, leaving them with a tingling feeling.

Amy's cunt tightened up then and her thrusting became somewhat awkward as her muscles seized. He opened his eyes and saw the look of pure ecstasy on her face as the orgasm was about to break. Amy held her breath, then let it out in a squeal of relief as the tension fled her and tingles of pleasure rippled through her being.

"Oh God," she gasped and squealed again. She sucked in a quick breath and repeated the words twice more before relaxing and flopping forward into his arms. Kyle nuzzled her neck and lightly bit into the soft flesh, making her shiver again. "That was such a nice orgasm," she whispered.

Their lips came together then and parted to allow the deployment of eager tongues. Amy's was lovely and wet and Kyle sucked the saliva from it. At the same time his hands gripped the cheeks of her ass very tightly and he thrust into her with short, sharp jabs of his cock. They kissed and fucked like this for a few more minutes, then Kyle peeled his mouth off hers.

"I wanna get on top of you now," he said and rolled her onto her back.

"Fuck me," she gasped and bucked against his thrusts.

Kyle put his shoulders behind her knees, effectively pushing her legs right back and opening her up for a damned good pounding.

His lengthy cock slid in and out of her with ease. Not that she was loose, just so well-lubricated. Her pussy sucked on his cock as he fucked her and his balls slapped against her firm ass. Amy clutched his upper arms and occasionally bucked against his strokes, causing him to plunge in deep and very hard. Each time she did this she gasped really loudly and would throw her head back.

Loving the sight of his cock stretching her wet cunt lips apart, Kyle entertained himself by watching his cock slide in and out of her. He found the look of it both fascinating and extremely stimulating.

"Keep going…like that," she said to him, "and you'll…make me come."

Loving the sound of that, Kyle increased his tempo by going up a gear while maintaining a steady rhythm, thrusting his dick in all the way with every stroke. He had her panting out of control now, and judging by the way her fingers were digging into his arms, she was getting very close to reaching another climax.

"Here it comes," she announced, an almost imploring look in her eyes.

Kyle loved the expressions she got on her face when she orgasmed, and right now was no different. He thumped into her cunt as hard as he could, knowing that this drove her absolutely wild when she was coming. Amy thrashed around on top of the bed, making a complete mess of the sheets. She reached behind him and grabbed his ass cheeks, where she roughly gouged the flesh with her nails. Her climax finished with a tremendous shudder and she lay still, gasping for breath. Kyle stopped thrusting and lightly kissed her on the lips.

"That was awesome," she said and smiled, her eyelids half closed and heavy with desire.

"I love it when you come," he told her. "It's a turn on."

She nodded. "For me as well, just quietly."

He grinned. "Yeah, I figured that."

They maneuvered into a sixty nine position so Amy could swallow his cock while Kyle gratefully tasted her wet and very delicious cunt. Juice coated his tongue and trickled into his mouth, satiating the thirst in his parched throat. Meanwhile, Amy was totally gorging his cock, thrusting her head down his length, driving his cock deep down her hungry throat.

She mounted him again then, desperate for his dick to be inside her once more. This time she rode him reverse cowgirl and Kyle played with her butt cheeks as she went up and down with fluid precision. One hand kept herself propped up while the other fondled his ball sack.

"These need to be emptied," she said, referring to his balls. "Do you think you can come with me riding you like this?"

"Yes," he was very quick to answer. "Just keep going the way you are and I'll get there."

Kyle lay back and enjoyed the ride. He put his hands behind his head and closed his eyes, focusing all his attention on the sensations happening down below, that exquisite feel of his girlfriend's soft cunt massaging his rigid shaft. Already he could feel the slight stirrings of impending ejaculation circulating through his loins. Those tingles rapidly intensified until his cock went super rigid, preparing to erupt.

He grunted loudly as he released his load deep inside Amy's waiting pussy. He filled her passage completely until his cum starting leaking from her lips. Amy kept thrusting until she was sure he was spent, then she relaxed and just sat on top of his cock.

"I really needed that," he grunted from behind her.

"I'm sure you did, Babe."

After a quick freshen up in the bathroom they got comfortable in bed with just the subtle light of a bedside lamp glowing in the room. Amy snuggled in close and Kyle tightly wrapped his arms around her.

"You know, I was thinking," Amy began.

"That could be dangerous," Kyle joked, for which he received a firm slap on the thigh.

"We've always had an open relationship," Amy continued on, "but lately we haven't indulged that freedom."

"You feeling the need to sleep with another man again?"

"Yes, but not one-on-one. I'd like us to find someone suitable and have a threesome. And then, after we've done that, find a girl for you and have another threesome." She propped herself up so she could look into his eyes. "What do you think?"

"You're right, it's been a while since we shared our love around. I'm up for it."

"Cool," Amy sounded happy. "Now we just need to find some sexy candidates."

* * *

Kyle and Amy were just finishing off dinner at a seafood restaurant. Kyle spooned the last mouthful of Crème Brule from the bowl and ate it.

"What about that guy you were doing a year or so ago?" Kyle suggested.

The pair had been struggling to find a male candidate to join them for the first of their proposed threesomes.

"I called him," Amy said, "but he has a steady girlfriend now. And there's no way she'd be agreeable to let him do something like that."

Kyle nodded. "Fair enough. We might have to go out to a bar or club and see if we can pick someone up."

"You might be right. The only interest we've had so far on that adult dating site is from complete losers. There's no one on there that

I'd consider opening my legs for."

"It's a shame," Kyle said with a shrug. "Seems like it should be a good convenient way of hooking up with someone, but obviously it sucks."

Amy frowned and sipped from a glass of water. "It seems much harder to hook up now than it was the last time we did this."

Kyle nodded in agreement." We'll find someone." He dabbed his lips on a napkin and signalled the waiter for the bill. When that was taken care of he grasped his girlfriend's hand and led her outside, where they took an evening stroll to walk off dinner.

"It's such a beautiful night," Amy said while gazing up at the stars. She slipped her arm around his waist and Kyle put his arm over her slender shoulders. "Why don't we duck into a bar for a drink and see what happens? It's not like we have anything else to do."

"Sure."

They took their time walking the few blocks into the center of town in search of some night life. It was a week night, so things were fairly quiet. Still, it wouldn't hurt to have a drink. If anything else came of that, then that would be a bonus.

"Let's go in here," Amy said and literally dragged her boyfriend off the street and into a quiet and ambient little bar. Inside were several couples, as well as a few men drinking alone. "He looks all right," she said, her eye on a man with short dark hair dressed in a suit and sipping on a glass of wine.

At the bar Kyle ordered a couple of red wines and they took a seat at a table near the man in question. He briefly glanced their way and

Amy offered him her best smile. His return smile was more like a grimace, looking rather uncomfortable that she was openly flirting with him when she obviously had a partner.

"Hi," Amy said brightly.

"Hi," he replied over his shoulder.

"Why don't you go talk to him alone and line him up," Kyle suggested in a quiet tone. "I'll just sit here and enjoy my drink."

Amy picked up her glass of wine and switched tables, pulling up a seat very close to the stranger. He appeared quite surprised by her actions, but readily indulged in conversation with her. Kyle watched on with some amusement as his girlfriend worked on picking the man up. He'd seen her do it before, but not recently. There was no jealousy in their relationship when it came to desires of the flesh. They had started off having an open relationship which they indulged regularly. It had only been in the last year where that facet of their love life had diminished.

Fifteen minutes later and Amy turned to Kyle and signalled him to come join them.

"This is my partner, Kyle," Amy said to the other man. To Kyle, she said, "And this is Rod." The two men shook hands and Kyle sat down. Amy grinned a little wickedly. "Rod is very interested in our proposal." She chuckled then. "Just so long as there is nothing gay going on."

Now it was Kyle's turn to laugh. "No problems there," he was adamant. "I'm not into guys."

Rod's relief was obvious. "Glad to hear it," he said.

"So, you're up for it?" Kyle asked in a low, conspiratorial voice. "Amy needs two hard dicks."

Rod nodded. "I've done this once before. When do you want to do this?"

Amy answered the question. "Are you free tonight?"

The man eyed them both in turn and nodded. He looked a touch apprehensive, but there was a distinct glint of excitement in his eyes at the same time.

Rod followed their car back to their house and, once inside, Amy poured everyone a glass of chilled white wine. The three took up seats in the living room; Kyle in an armchair while Amy and Rod sat close together on the couch. Kyle watched with interest as his girlfriend flirted with Rod. The man still looked a little stiff, but soon started to loosen up.

"You're sure this is okay?" he asked Kyle the question. "Me having sex with your girl?"

Kyle shrugged nonchalantly. "Sure. We've done this before. It's no problem." He grinned. "After Amy's had two men tonight, next time it's my turn to have two women…And I can't tell you how much I'm looking forward to that." To Amy, he said, "Why don't you strip naked, Babe, and show Rod your hot little body."

"Okay," Amy sounded excited.

She put her glass of wine on the coffee table and made a bit of a show of shedding her dress, followed by bra, then lastly her panties. Rod's eyes kept roaming all over her naked flesh, paying particular attention to her big tits and luscious cunt.

"That looks tasty," he said, referring to her shaven vagina.

"It is," Kyle assured the man.

"And I'm soaking wet right now," Amy said to Rod. She pushed him flat on his back and straddled his face, dropping her steaming cunt down onto his open mouth. She sighed and her eyelids immediately grew heavy with desire when Rod started to feed on her pussy. "That feels so fucking nice, Rod," she complimented him. "I hope you like the taste of me."

Kyle saw the man nod vigorously and grunt as he fed on Amy's mound. Amy rocked back and forth on his face, panting and moaning the entire time he licked her wet slit. Kyle's cock was throbbing inside his pants as he watched the action on the lounge. He gave his member a rub, then took off his shirt and kicked off his shoes. Standing up he dropped his pants and underwear and sat back down completely naked. Gently he stroked his own cock, biding his time before joining the others, for now just content to be a voyeur rather than a participant.

While Rod continued to feast on Amy's cunt, Amy managed to undo his pants and slip them partway down his thighs, exposing a sizeable and very thick cock. Kyle saw the look of immense satisfaction on her face when she first set eyes on Rod's big prick. She jerked on it while Rod busily tongued her passage. They were both grunting and groaning now. Rod paused and sucked in air as Amy leaned forward and took the head of his dick into her mouth.

"Fuck!" he exclaimed and buried his face in her pussy again.

Amy sucked the man hard and furiously, driving his shaft down her wanton throat relentlessly. Meanwhile, Kyle continued to jerk on his own member, nearing the point where he would need to feed it into either Amy's mouth or her wet cunt.

The sixty niner on the lounge continued on for a few more minutes. Eventually Amy got off Rod and he stood up so he could undress completely. While he did this Kyle left his seat and perched himself at one end of the couch. His girlfriend got on all fours on the cushions and took Kyle's cock into her mouth. By now Rod was nude and he just stood there watching Amy go down on Kyle.

"Get in behind her and fuck her," Kyle told the man. "She's gagging for it." As he said those last words Amy gagged on his cock when she deep-throated him. Kyle grinned and looked at Rod as he prepared to enter Amy's cunt. "See. Gagging for it."

Amy spat Kyle out and gasped with pleasure when Rod thudded deep into her cunt with one very aggressive thrust.

"Fuck me hard and deep," she said and engulfed Kyle's prick once more.

Rod *did* give her a good pounding, thrusting into her with bludgeoning strokes of his immense dick. Amy was groaning out of control, but she never let up on sucking Kyle's cock while being fucked doggie by her ring-in lover. Kyle knew from past experience just how much she enjoyed having a cock in her mouth and cunt at the same time.

She took him deep down her throat while Rod fucked her nice and deep. Amy's hand jerked Kyle's shaft as she ravaged the sensitive head. She spat him out then and ran her tongue down his length, squeezed his balls together with her hand and sucked them both into her mouth at the same time.

"That feel so awesome, Babe," he told her. He then asked Rod, "How's her pussy feel?"

"Bloody fantastic," Rod was excited, his eyes glued to the spectacle of his cock disappearing inside Amy's cunt. "She's very tight. And so damned wet."

"I know," said Kyle. "Amy's got a fantastic little pussy. Can't wait to fuck it again myself."

Rod stopped thrusting. "Do you want a turn now?"

Kyle shook his head. "Not yet, man. You've gotta make her come first. Then I'll take over."

He just leaned back and relaxed as his woman went to town on his cock. The harder Rod fucked her the harder she sucked it. Kyle thrust into her mouth very rapidly for a spell, then relaxed again and fantasized about the threesome with two women that he would experience in the near future. It had been a while and he could not wait.

"I'm…gonna…come!" Amy gasped and let out a howl of delight as an orgasm swept over her. Rod pounded her senseless from the rear, his flesh smacking against her butt as he plundered her hard with his meaty dick. "Oh, God!...Oh, God!" she squealed as a series of shivers and shudders went through her.

"Keep going," Kyle urged Rod. "She's not quite done yet. There's a bit more in her."

Rod heeded his words and continued to give her a good rogering until he was certain her orgasm had completely subsided. Only then did he stop and pull out of her.

"I want you to ride me," Kyle said to Amy. "Rod? You sit next to me so Amy can lean over and take your dick deep down her throat while she's on my lap."

Kyle waited for Amy to mount him and sighed with relief when he felt himself sink deep into her sizzling wetness. The firmness of her cunt around his cock was divine, a sensation that was heavily accentuated when she started going up and down. When she was into a rhythm she leaned to her left and sampled Rod's rod once again. Now the other man sighed with pleasure.

She was very, very flexible and a bit of an expert at doing two things at the same time. Amy didn't miss a beat in fucking Kyle while bent over to consume Rod's throbbing erection. Both her pussy and mouth made wet noises as she worked diligently away on the two men simultaneously.

"You're like the ultimate fuck, Babe," Kyle said emphatically, admiring her efforts and obvious skills. He spanked her ass really hard several times, then took a hold of one of her breasts and twisted the hardened nipple. "Suck his cock deep down your throat," he told her while exhilarating in the way her pussy slid up and down his aching shaft.

When Amy came again she paused in going down on Rod so she could tilt her head back and howl at the ceiling. She bounced up and down furiously as fresh juice flooded her passage and gushed out onto Kyle's balls. She thrashed about on top of him for another minute or so, then sat still and gasped for breath until she'd relaxed.

Amy spoke up. "Rod? I want you to come round behind me now and slip that big cock into my ass while Kyle stays in my pussy."

Rod didn't hesitate for even a second. Eager for more penetration, he got in behind Amy while she leaned well forward. Amy jerked and groaned as his hefty length slipped into her ass an inch at a time.

She couldn't help but grin. "That feels so fucking good, guys. Two huge cocks at once is every girl's dream."

As Rod rather gently thrust into her ass, Amy started to move her hips as well and managed to get into a synchronized rhythm with Rod. Kyle just sat back and relaxed while he was ridden yet again. Occasionally he felt Rod's balls brush against his, but he tried to ignore that. It was merely collateral in this kind of position. Couldn't be helped.

"Both my cunt and ass are on fire," Amy said and swooned, her eyes rolling back in her head.

"You're gonna have a hell of an orgasm this time," Kyle noted and roughly squeezed her beautiful boobs. He felt like kissing her, but wasn't keen on that after recently having another man's cock in her mouth. She was too squashed up against him for Kyle to be able to taste her breasts, so in order to give his mouth something to do he bit into her soft neck and gave her a hickey.

Rod was really giving her anal passage a good reaming now, causing Amy to rock back and forth on Kyle's cock. Something about the angle was really rubbing the head of his dick and he felt the first early stirrings of ejaculation. Quickly he put his mind onto boring, mundane chores at work until the urge had passed.

"Fuck me!" Amy suddenly screamed. "Fucking give it to me!"

Rod literally hammered her from the rear now, plundering her tighter passage with his massive girth. Kyle himself was unable to do much of anything. To help out he seized his girlfriend by the ass and dragged her up and down his cock while Rod continued to bury himself in her ass.

"I'm getting close," she announced and sucked in a quick breath. "My ass is burning up. This is gonna be mind-blowing."

"Come all over our cocks, Babe," Kyle implored her. "I wanna hear you screaming."

Even before she exploded Amy started to scream. Her body trembled as the tension built and she screamed again when the climax finally broke. She rocked madly back and forth on top of Kyle, and Rod didn't slow down in his thrusting. Amy's nails clawed at Kyle's back, threatening to draw blood. She gasped and moaned and trembled some more, then let out yet another ear-piercing screech. Her orgasm seemed to go on for minutes before it started to abate, leaving her a shivering mess sandwiched between her two lovers.

"Oh my fucking goodness," she whispered hoarsely. "That was one of the most intense orgasms I've ever had." She broke into a rather tired grin then. "I think I'm fucked."

"Maybe you should take a short break," Kyle suggested. "Rod and I aren't finished with you yet."

"I know. You boys need to come too." Rod slipped out of her ass and Amy got to her feet. "Let's have another wine, then get back into it."

She disappeared into the kitchen and returned with a fresh bottle of wine and set about refilling the three empty glasses. Rod was sweating a little from his efforts and he quickly drank half his glass. Amy kissed him on the cheek.

"You having a good time?" she asked their guest.

"I'm having a great fucking time," he said and laughed.

After the wines Kyle moved the coffee table out of the way and indicated for Amy to get down on all fours on the fluffy white rug. Rod sat down on the floor with his back against the lounge and Amy sucked his now-flaccid dick back to full hardness. Kyle jerked his own cock while watching the display. When he was erect once more he got in behind his girlfriend and spent a moment probing the entrance to her cunt with the head of his cock. She was still very wet and soon he grew too impatient to tease her any longer. He buried the head of his shaft into her lips, grabbed her by the hips and gave one powerful thrust that drove his length all the way inside her until the head nudged the very end of her succulent passage.

Amy gasped and almost choked on Rod's cock. She wanked it in her hand for a moment before plunging it down her throat again while her boyfriend got into a steady rhythm behind her.

Kyle alternated between watching his cock disappear in her cunt and Rod's dick disappearing inside her mouth. Both visuals were a complete turn on. Her pussy flooded with fresh juice now that he was giving it a good fucking and he loved the way it really squeezed his shaft.

He spanked her ass once on each cheek, thrust into her rapidly, then smacked her butt again. Each time he did this Amy emitted a garbled squeal with a mouthful of cock. Kyle stroked her with long, deep strokes. To mix things up a little he occasionally gave her short strokes that barely penetrated a few inches inside her hungry lips.

"Suck his fucking big cock," Kyle seethed as he continued to plunge into Amy's desperate cunt. "Suck the hot cum from his balls and swallow it."

Rod grinned when he heard Kyle's words. The man's face was a picture of concentration and Kyle could tell Rod was focused on unloading down Amy's throat. Kyle knew Amy would savor every milky drop of Rod's jiz. She loved swallowing cum.

Kyle decided to go for his own glory now and empty his balls inside Amy's passage. He thrust into her hard and fast, all his attention now trained on releasing his seed. He felt the tingles start to form in his loins and rapidly intensify. His body jerked and his cock stiffened even further a moment before the cum exploded from his dick and drowned Amy's cunt.

No sooner had he come when Rod started grunting. His face contorted and he let out a sigh as he started ejaculating into Amy's waiting mouth. She greedily swallowed his load and finished with a satisfied smack of her lips.

Kyle pulled out and sat back on the rug, suddenly feeling extremely relaxed. Rod appeared equally as content.

"I'm really glad I went out for a drink tonight," Rod said and grinned.

* * *

The following evening after a bout of one-on-one sex, Amy and Kyle sat at the computer in their bedroom sipping from a glass of wine each. They were on the adult dating site where they had, rather surprisingly, acquired the interest of an attractive female.

"I like the sound of her," Kyle commented while reading her messages and profile information again.

"And the look of her, I'm sure," Amy said knowingly. She broke into a smile then and kissed him on the cheek.

"Ask her if she'd like to meet up for a threesome."

"That might be a little forward just now."

"We already know she's interested in one," Kyle insisted. "Just put it on her."

Amy nodded, took a sip of wine, then typed up a short message asking the young woman if she'd be keen to meet up in the near future for some play time. Then they waited for her to respond. She did, less than a minute later.

Kyle grinned with excitement when he read her message. This time she gave her real name, which was April.

"You were right," said Amy. "She is keen to fuck us."

"She sounds even keener than we are," said Kyle.

Another message came through then with April stating she has a fantasy to do it outdoors in the daytime in an open field somewhere, and she was keen to do it within the next few days, preferably on the weekend.

Kyle ducked out to the kitchen and refilled their glasses. When he returned he and Amy discussed a possible meet up place and time, then messaged April again with some details. It was a few minutes before she replied, agreeing to meet them there at ten in the morning. She also sent through her cell phone number. Amy sent a quick reply with her number as well and the deal was done.

Rubbing his hands together with glee, Kyle said, "I can't wait to have a threesome with two hot chicks. It's been so long."

Amy rubbed his chest. "I know, Baby. You need one. You deserve it." She grinned. "I so enjoyed the other night with you and Rod." She shrugged. "I'm looking forward to getting with a girl again, too."

Although Kyle wouldn't have labeled Amy full-on bisexual, she did enjoy the attentions of a female from time to time. And giving attention to a woman. He was getting a raging hard-on just thinking about it. Saturday was only two days away, but it seemed like forever. He felt like fucking this delicious April girl tonight.

"I'm horny again," he told his girlfriend. "I know we only had sex a little while ago, but how about a very quick fuck before bed?"

"Sure, Babe," Amy was agreeable. "I could use one more orgasm myself."

They were both already naked, so it was simply a matter of climbing into bed and getting right into it. Kyle just got on top and fucked her missionary, planning on waiting until she came once, and then going for his own climax.

"Your cock feels so good, Babe," Amy crooned. Her eyes were shut and the hint of a satisfied smile curled the corners of her mouth.

"It goes in so deep, and I love the feel of your balls slapping against my ass cheeks."

They tongued then, wet and very sensually. What was it about kissing, Kyle wondered, that was such a turn on? Her tongue thrust deep into his mouth and his fought for space in hers. All the while his cock hammered into her wet cunt like a love machine. They both gasped and moaned as they tongued.

Suddenly Kyle stopped kissing her and exclaimed, "Fuck I love fucking your tight little cunt!"

"Fuck it then," Amy demanded. "Fuck it really hard and make it come."

"I'm going to."

Kyle plunged into her like a jack hammer and had her squealing with ecstasy. Her nails clawed at the skin of his back, his butt and his arms. Amy writhed around on the sheets, occasionally bucking against his thrusts and driving his cock in very deep. Her cunt was welcoming and massaged his shaft with a spongy, loving embrace.

"I'm...gonna...come," she announced and let out the longest of moans. Her eyes clamped tightly closed. Amy went through the pleasurable throes of orgasm, panting and moaning out of control. Again her nails dug into his flesh, so hard it was painful. Just as her orgasm started to subside, Kyle felt his own coming on fast.

"Oh...fuck!" he grunted as he squirted his hot load inside her greedy pussy. "Fuck!" he said again.

"Tongue me," Amy urged.

They kissed feverishly as Kyle continued to unleash his seed. He sighed into her mouth, then relaxed, his tongue caressing hers.

* * *

Saturday finally arrived. Both Kyle and Amy dressed casually in shorts and T-shirts. Amy didn't bother wearing a bra. A large picnic blanket was put in the boot of the car and they were off, driving through the suburbs and out into the countryside.

"Do you think she'll show up?" Amy asked out of the blue.

Kyle guided the car slowly around a sharp left-hand bend.

"I fucking hope so," he said. "I'm keen as hell for this threesome." He nodded as the road straightened up. "No. She'll be there."

He felt Amy's hand on his thigh and he glanced at her with a smile. She smiled back, her hair billowing about her face with the convertible's top down.

The sun was out and the skies were clear, apart from a few sporadic patches of fluffy white cloud. The day was warm without being hot and there was no chance of inclement weather.

Kyle turned right and stopped at the end of the short road. Armed with the blanket the pair wandered into the forest, following a well-used trail. When they arrived at a pile of boulders, they turned right, trekking a short distance through the forest until it opened up into a lush field of short grass with just several large trees to offer some shade. Amy and Kyle headed for one of those trees and spread out the blanket in the shade. They were a little early, so they sat down on the blanket to await April's arrival.

She ended up being a slightly late. Amy was the first to spot her emerging from the forest and start walking across the field. The young woman's blonde hair shimmered in the sunlight. She was also dressed very casually in denim shorts and a red tank top. As she drew nearer Kyle felt his excitement growing. He loved this kind of situation, where they were about to get down and dirty with a complete stranger. It was a weird scenario in a way, but highly arousing.

"Hi," Amy greeted April brightly.

The two girls hugged like old friends. April embraced Kyle, then stepped back to eye her two soon-to-be lovers up and down. She smiled with approval after her appraisal.

"Is this your first time doing something like this?" Amy asked the woman as the three sat down and shared sips from a bottle of water.

April shook her pretty head. "No. I'm somewhat of a veteran when it comes to meeting in strange places for sex. Guess I'd be termed a bit of a slut, but I just love sex and I like variety." She smiled again and looked at each of them in turn. "I love doing couples. I enjoy both men and women."

"So do I," Amy said.

"I just like women," Kyle was adamant. "No bisexual tendencies in me, that's for sure."

"Do you guys do this sort of thing often?" April wanted to know.

"We used to," Kyle answered.

"But we've been very quiet of late," Amy put in. "We just decided a few days ago that we were going to get back into a more swinging lifestyle." She then went on to describe the threesome with

Rod in great detail and Kyle could see it was getting April quite horny. He could see the lust building in her eyes.

He slipped his shirt off and exposed his fit torso. He wasn't particularly muscular or ripped like someone who frequented the gym, but he was in pretty good shape. As expected April's eyes looked over his body and a smile curled her mouth again. When Amy took off her top and revealed her luscious boobs, April's eyes then roamed her flesh.

"Your turn," Amy said and April removed her own top.

Kyle could no longer resist. He moved in close to April, took a breast in each hand, felt the nipples stiffen into his palms and kissed her on the lips. Her arms wrapped around his neck as she thrust her eager tongue into his mouth. Kyle's cock sprang to life and immediately throbbed. Next thing he knew his girlfriend's hands were busy down there, first fondling it through his shorts, then undoing his shorts and setting it free. Now completely naked, his lips still locked on April's, he felt Amy's wet lips encircle the head as she started to suck.

Kyle broke the kiss and said to April, "Help her out down there." He then lay back, closed his eyes and just savored the ecstasy of experiencing two beautiful women keenly sucking on his cock.

He could hear constant wet, slurping sounds as the girls continually swapped his cock from mouth to mouth. Hands were everywhere, as were lips and tongues. Not only was his cock pleasured, but also his balls. They were sucked and licked and played with by wandering fingers. He heard the girls kiss, so he looked up.

Their kiss was open-mouthed with lots of tongue. April stroked his wet and aching cock as she kissed Amy, her actions sending delicious tingles through his body. Amy's fingers toyed with his sack, adding to the stimulation.

"Fuck that feels good," he groaned rather loudly. "I've been dying for this."

"Bet you can't wait to feel April's hot, wet pussy wrapped around your dick," Amy said with a grin, then wrestled the cock from April and swallowed it once more.

April just played with Kyle's balls and let Amy suck for a while. She looked up at Kyle's face and offered him a gorgeous smile. There was a twinkle in her eyes and Kyle could almost read her thoughts. She was keen as to feel his throbbing cock deep inside her horny cunt.

While Amy continued to deep-throat him, April kissed her way up Kyle's body, pausing for a moment to suck on one of his nipples. Then her wet mouth was pressed against his and her tongue was darting between his lips. Kyle grabbed a hold of her head and pashed her furiously, hungry as hell for this woman's affections. Amy was going crazy on his cock, sucking and slurping, jerking it roughly in her fist and sometimes lashing her restless tongue all over his testicles. He peeled his lips away from April's.

"I'm so fucking horny right now," he gasped. "Put one of your tits in my mouth."

When April grabbed a boob and guided a rubbery nipple into his open mouth, Kyle gasped with pleasure again and sucked it hard as once again he felt his length slip deep down his girlfriend's hot throat.

Kyle spat the nipple out and said, "I really need to fuck someone."

"You go first," Amy said to April while holding Kyle's dick in an upright position. "Come down here and sit on it while I feed it into you."

April stripped off her shorts and straddled his hips, where she lowered her steaming pussy onto the head of his cock. Amy fed it into her inch by inch until his entire member was enveloped by her hot wetness. April gasped and commenced moving up and down his shank while Amy stripped naked and sat on Kyle's face. His tongue was greeted with a river of warm, sweet juice and he was only too happy to suck some down his parched throat. And the feeling of April's exquisitely tight pussy sliding up and down his cock felt amazing.

He grabbed a hold of Amy's butt cheeks and thrashed his tongue inside her. She rocked back and forth on his mouth, grinding her cunt hard against his lips and nose. She was panting with sexual heat and so was April.

The other girl was bouncing around on top of his dick like crazy now, and Kyle suspected she was rapidly building up for a very explosive orgasm. He loved it when a girl came on his cock, knowing that it was his dick, and/or his technique that had got them off.

To his surprise Amy came before April did. Juice flooded her cunt when the climax struck and Kyle thrust his tongue in deep to capture as much of her cum as he could. Amy ground her pussy down onto his mouth and squealed. A moment later April added her own notes to the symphony as she reached a climax as well.

When Amy rolled off his face, Kyle sucked in some deep breaths and watched April's cute little ass bounce up and down as she continued to pound him. When her orgasm had finished Amy wrestled his dick out of the other girl's pussy and thrust it deep down her throat to suck the juices from it. April joined in the feast and enthusiastically took a turn deep-throating him as well.

"Oh…Fuck!" Kyle bellowed and put a hand on the back of April's head, holding her mouth down on his cock. Amy then brushed his hand away, placed both of her hands on April's skull and pushed her up and down like a pump. "That feels so fucking intense. You take a turn again, Babe, and April can push down on your head." The girls switched and did as Kyle suggested, April roughly forcing down on Amy's head and driving Kyle's cock all the way down her throat. "Your turn to ride it," he said to Amy. "April? Come and sit that sweet little pussy down onto my face."

Eager for more action, the girls quickly got into position. Amy first sank her pussy down his shaft while facing him and April sat on his face facing Amy. As Kyle tongued that delicious young, fresh cunt, he heard the girls tongue one another. Amy rose and fell slowly on his cock while April just sat still on his face and let Kyle do his thing down there. The girls continued to pash, stifled pants and moans increasing with fervency with every passing second. Amy bounced harder and Amy started to grind on his lips and tongue. Kyle wanted both women to come again and he was pretty sure they both would.

God, April's cunt tasted divine! So wet and so fucking sweet. He tongued her passage with venom, loving the way the fluids kept replenishing themselves every time he greedily drank some. Her lips were very smooth and freshly waxed. He sucked on them, tongue-lashed her clitoris, then sank his tongue back into her searing tunnel.

Amy was thumping herself down onto his cock now, driving him in very deep and massaging every inch of her beautiful and very tight corridor. Still he could hear the girls kissing with intense passion. Constant muffled moans could be heard and Kyle sensed they were getting very close to a climax.

In perfect timing both women came simultaneously. April bounced up and down on his tongue while Amy bludgeoned herself on his prick. Cunt juice was everywhere now, all over his face, trickling down his chin, his cock, all over his shaven ball sack. The air was filled with the sounds of two young ladies gripped by sexual ecstasy. The orgasms seemed to go on and on. More juice flowed from both aroused passages. Kyle sucked April's into his mouth and drank it while Amy's well overflowed onto his groin. Eventually both climaxes subsided and the girls hopped off his face and cock, leaving Kyle there gasping for air.

Leaving him out of the equation for the moment so they could fully indulge their bisexual tendencies, the women got into a sixty niner with Amy lying prone and April on top. Kyle smiled as he watched the dual cunnilingus action and slowly stroked his wet cock. Soon he would get behind April and give her a damned good fucking, but right now he was content to just watch for a minute or two.

"That looks so hot," he commented as the girls ground their

pussies against each other's faces.

Kyle soon ran out of patience. He needed to fuck again, so he got in behind April and entered her cunt with one aggressive thrust. As he slowly stroked her cavern, Amy continued to lick the other girl's clit. Occasionally she flicked her tongue either over Kyle's balls, or licked juice from his shaft as he exited April's tunnel. At one stage Kyle withdrew all the way and thrust his member into Amy's gaping mouth. She sucked it hard, then he fed it back into April, much to her delight.

He watched his cock disappearing inside their ring-in lover. The sight of his girlfriend's pretty face down there between April's legs was also one hell of a turn on. Amy smiled up at him and Kyle smiled back. They were both having a great time and no doubt April was as well.

"Fuck her, Babe," Amy said and gasped as the other girl's tongue slipped deep inside her hot cunt.

Kyle fucked her like a machine, sliding in and out more and more rapidly. April's snatch was so tight it was sending tingles all through him and made him want to come. He slowed his pace a little and thought about something else temporarily until things were back under control.

"I'm gonna come," April said and let our a scream as the orgasm sent her body into a series of trembles.

Kyle took Amy missionary next, kneeling between her outstretched legs as April planted her flowering pussy onto Amy's waiting mouth. Kyle took the opportunity to tongue April while he fucked his partner with short, sharp strokes. When he was done kissing her, his mouth ventured lower until he was taking turns sucking on each of her peachy tits. April used her hands to squeeze them together for him so he could lash his eager tongue over both nipples at the same time.

"Make her come," April said to Kyle, her tone bordering on demanding.

"I plan to," he murmured as he devoured a breast.

Kyle stopped playing with April and focused on bringing his girl to another climax. It took less than a minute of fast, deep and concentrated strokes to get her there, and when she exploded she gripped onto April's thighs tightly and screamed into the other girl's cunt. Kyle pulled out when she was done and sat back on the blanket to stretch his cramping legs.

"Let's make Kyle come," April said then, a gleam of excitement and anticipation in her blue eyes. The girls converged on him and started licking his cock and balls all over. "I wanna see him squirt his beautiful sperm everywhere."

The women sucked his dick for a moment, then April got into a rhythm with her hand while Amy just looked on. Kyle was on his back, but propped up on his elbows so he could watch. He focused his attention on releasing his load, and soon it was spewing forth from the eye of his cock and splashing all over his torso, leaving him drenched in a milky sea. Both girls grinned and April giggled excitedly as she watched him ejaculate. She sampled some off his skin then and fed it to Amy in a wet kiss.

Kyle lay back and stared up at the azure sky, smiling with contentment.

It was so great to be back into the swing of their open relationship.

Caught in the Act

Jimmy was at home getting ready to go out. He finished off with a generous spray of cologne and checked his hair in the mirror for about the tenth time. He was about to leave the bathroom when he decided to gargle some mouthwash. Once that was done he figured her was set.

He was on his way to visit his new girlfriend at her place. Girlfriend of sorts, anyway. They'd only been seeing each other a couple of weeks, but things had been going quite well and the sex was great.

Sandy didn't live far from him, just five minutes away in the next suburb. He parked his car out front, once again checked his appearance in the rearview mirror and got out. He was feeling randy tonight and hoped she was in the mood for a bit of fun. She should be. Seemed pretty keen.

After knocking on the door Jimmy waited. Lights were on inside and he could hear music playing at a relatively low volume. A moment later the door swung open to reveal a smiling Sandy. She had medium brown hair with some highlights throughout. Her pale brown eyes gave him the once over, then her arms were around his neck and she was kissing him deeply.

Things were looking good so far, Jimmy thought as he tongued her back.

"Come in," she said. "I have a beer waiting for you."

Jimmy grinned. "You must be the perfect woman."

Sandy laughed. "Don't get too used to it."

He tailed her into the living room. She was dressed in a summery white dress that hung loosely on her body. Jimmy could see the outline of her underwear through the thin material. In the living room the TV was on, but the volume muted. The iPod dock was playing a track he'd never heard before. Wasn't really his kind of music, but hey, it was her house. True to her word a tall glass of icy beer sat on a coaster on the coffee table near the lounge. They both sat down and Sandy picked up a glass of wine while Jimmy immediately sampled the brew.

"Nice," he said.

"It's your favorite brand," she told him.

"You truly are the perfect woman," he repeated his earlier comment. He nodded towards the iPod dock. "What are we listening to?"

Sandy shrugged. "I don't know, actually. I just downloaded a couple of obscure tracks last night for something different. Do you like it?"

Now it was his turn to shrug. "It's okay."

"I can play something else if you like."

"No. This is fine. It's good background music." He patted her on the leg. "So, how's your day been?"

"Work was okay. Nothing special. Just glad to be home and relaxing. I've been looking forward to you coming over tonight."

Jimmy turned to her and smiled. "Any particular reason why?"

"I enjoy your company." Now she smiled, her eyes gleaming. "And that other thing that's obviously on your mind right now."

"Does that mean I'll be getting lucky?"

"I think sex was always going to be on the cards." She nodded at the glass in his hand. "But you have to finish your drink first."

Jimmy took his time. There was no rush. He didn't want this girl to think he was just here for that. He liked her, liked chatting to her and just hanging out with her.

When they'd both drained their glasses, Sandy took his from him and placed both of them on the coffee table. She started to kiss him and helped him out of his shirt. Inside his pants Jimmy's member was pulsing with energy and pure lust. He couldn't wait to get it out and have it played with. When Sandy started to undo his pants, he stopped her.

"What?" she said, eyeing him quizzically.

"Is your flat mate home?"

"No. Moira's out."

"What if she comes back and we're doing it on the couch? Maybe we should go into your bedroom?"

"She's spending the night at a friend's house. She won't be back."

Sandy continued to strip him of his pants and removed his underwear as well. Jimmy was now completely nude and it felt good to be so. Free. He watched as she pulled her dress off over her head. She wasn't wearing any bra and he could see her nipples were nice and aroused. Sandy tugged off her panties and tossed them onto the carpet. Again they embraced and kissed heatedly, their desire escalating with every lash of wet tongues.

Jimmy hand a hand on one of her breasts, where he eagerly kneaded and squeezed the soft flesh before paying particular attention to the stiff nipple. Sandy had gone straight for gold, holding his thick cock in a firm grasp. She didn't pump it or stroke it yet, just content to hang onto it for now as she ravenously tongued his mouth. Jimmy's hand wandered lower, lightly passing over her stomach and venturing down between her parted thighs. His middle finger slid over her clitoris and she shuddered with excitement. It went lower until it sank into the juicy wetness of her shaved pussy.

She stopped kissing him then so she could moan freely as he fingered her twat. Now her hand got busy on his cock and she started jerking it rather erratically.

"Fuck I'm horny," Jimmy said hoarsely, desire constricting his throat.

"I am too, just a little bit," Sandy conceded and grinned. "Put two fingers inside me." When he slipped in a second one she sighed heavily, closed her eyes, let go of his cock and reclined. "That feels so nice."

Jimmy pleasured her like this for a few minutes. Needing to do more than just finger her, he got down between her legs and starting licking her delicious little pussy. Her lower lips were so soft and smooth and very wet. He sucked on them, then sucked on her clit. Sandy continually gasped every time he did something, and panted incessantly when he rapidly tongued her cunt. He was quite noisy as he ate her, making loud sucking sounds with the occasional smacking of his lips. She was so tasty. He loved it.

"You're really getting me going," she swooned and ran her fingers through his short hair. "I think I might come soon."

Keen for her to do just that, Jimmy worked hard on her clit until he had her squirming around on the lounge and squealing in orgasm. When her climax had passed he sat up and wiped the moisture from his chin. Sandy just lay there, her eyes still closed and a satisfied smile on her face.

She suddenly pounced on him them and started gorging his cock down her throat, feeding on him like she was starving. Her hand worked his shank and played with his balls as she relentlessly drove him in and out of her mouth, sometimes deep down her throat.

There was the sound of the front door opening and closing, but Sandy didn't seem to notice. Jimmy roughly pulled her head away from his dick and grabbed a lounge cushion to cover his private parts.

Moira, her cute little brunette flat mate, entered the living room, saw the naked pair and dropped her jaw. She blushed, managed to compose herself and said, "Should I just go to my room and pretend I didn't see anything?"

"We didn't think you were coming home tonight," Sandy said.

"Obviously." Instead of disappearing to her room, Moira took a seat in a chair that angled towards the lounge. She sat there staring at them. "Well? Keep going? Don't let me spoil your fun."

Sandy said slowly, "You want to watch us?"

The other woman nodded. "Call me kinky, but this looks better than anything on television."

Jimmy giggled nervously, not sure if Moira was being serious or not. Sandy took the cushion away from his lap, exposing his still-erect member for all to see. He noticed Moira's eyes drop to his crotch and she didn't seem to mind having a good look at what he had down there.

To his surprise Sandy picked up where she'd left off and resumed sucking his cock, working it in and out of her lips like she had been before they were interrupted. Jimmy kept his eyes on Moira. She kept her eyes on the oral action. He saw the brunette lick her lips and he realized he might be in for something far more than he'd bargained for.

Now he couldn't believe his eyes as Moira opened her legs, pulled her panties aside and started playing with her pussy, rubbing her clit and plunging several fingers inside her tunnel. That visual, along with his girlfriend going down on him was enough to make him want to explode prematurely.

"Stop for a second," he said to Sandy and she pulled her head away. It was only then that she noticed her flat mate was fingering herself.

Sandy's next statement stunned him completely. "Would you like a turn?" she said to Moira.

Moira said nothing, just got out of her chair and knelt on the floor in front of Jimmy. Sandy held his cock out to her and Moira took the head into her mouth, where her tongue ran rings around it.

Jimmy couldn't believe this was happening and his head was

swimming with lust and desire.

The two young women took turns pleasuring his pole, stroking it, sucking it, licking up and down its length and playing with his balls like they were a bag of marbles. And the sounds their mouths were making was a huge turn on in itself.

"Suck it," he said. "Suck it really hard." He then specifically said to Sandy, "You don't mind Moira sucking my cock?"

Sandy shook her head and replied, "Not at all."

Jimmy started to wonder then whether this whole scenario had been planned; not just on Sandy's part, but by both girls. It all seemed too easy somehow. Whatever the deal was, he wasn't about to complain or put a stop to it. Hell, no! This was awesome!

The girls surprised him again when they paused in giving him head and spent a few minutes kissing right in front of him. Feeling the urge for some tongue action himself, Jimmy leaned forward, kissed Sandy, then had his first kiss from Moira. Both girls kissed quite beautifully.

"I need to be fucked," Sandy announced.

Jimmy had an idea. "Why don't I lie down and you can get on top. That way Moira can sit on my face if she wants."

Sandy glanced at Moira and the other woman nodded.

Keen, Jimmy quickly got prone on the lounge and watched as his girl mounted him cowgirl style. Facing her friend, Moira squatted on Jimmy's open mouth and his lips engulfed her sweet and very wet cunt. What a position. What a fantasy come true. One gorgeous pussy sliding up and down his cock while another was planted firmly on his hungry mouth. This was fantastic, the ultimate in stimulation.

The flat mates were both panting and moaning as their pussies were pleasured in different ways. Sandy was very adept at riding and she went quite hard, her nails digging into the flesh of his stomach as she pounded him into the lounge. Moira rocked gently on his face, making sure both her clitoris and passage received regular attention.

Sandy reached a climax first, thrashing about on top of him as she came. Jimmy felt her juices flooding out of her and flowing freely over his balls. He managed to bring Moira to orgasm less than a minute later. She filled his mouth with her cum and he swallowed every delicious, precious drop.

The girls got off him simultaneously. Jimmy sat up and put his feet on the floor.

Moira eyed his cock, then looked at Sandy. "Do you mind if I ride it?" she asked.

"Go for it," Sandy was readily agreeable. "But only if you ride him reverse cowgirl. That way I can get a great view."

Jimmy sighed with pleasure as Moira's pussy slid down his shaft until her lips were touching his balls. Sandy sat down on the carpet in front of them and looked on with fascination as Moira fucked her boyfriend.

"That looks hot," said Sandy.

Jimmy could only imagine how good it looked. It felt fantastic, and that was what he was concentrating on. He grabbed chunks of Moira's ass as she rose and fell. Her pussy gripped his shaft very tightly and she was soaking wet; wetter than she had been before her climax just before. He felt his girlfriend's hand on his sack then, followed by her lips and tongue. This was incredible. One girl fucking him while the other had her mouth all over his balls. Sandy wrenched his cock from Moira's cunt then and spent a good two minutes sucking it so intensely that Jimmy could barely sit still. Eventually she guided it back inside her flat mate's passage and Moira rode him until she came for the second time.

Jimmy did Sandy missionary on the lounge then while Moira sat on her face. Jimmy and Moira tongued for a while, both of them gasping and groaning during the kiss. Jimmy fucked his girl hard and deep and Sandy responded by thrashing Moira's clit with her tongue. He kissed Moira again, but very briefly this time. Moira was too focused on Sandy's tongue action to do any of her own.

Content to just concentrate on fucking his girlfriend, Jimmy stroked her pussy long and deep with great rhythm, so much so that he had her in the grip of yet another climax less than two minutes later. He pulled out of her when she was done and sat back on the lounge to rest a moment.

Moira immediately took advantage and fell forward, where she started tonguing Sandy's cunt, effectively maneuvering her way into a sixty-nine position.

"How hot does that look?" Jimmy stated emphatically as he took in the ultimate in eye candy. While he watched he slowly stroked his cock, but would have preferred it if one of the girls was doing it.

It took close to ten minutes before the girls had another climax and finally disentangled themselves from one another. Sandy looked at Jimmy and moved in next to him. She removed his hand from his dick and took it into her own grasp, where she proceeded to jerk him off in an expert fashion.

"I'm going to make you explode everywhere," she told him. "We want to see you cum. Put on a show for us girls."

Moira was now seated cross-legged on the floor so she could watch, her eyes wide with anticipation of seeing Jimmy shoot his load all over the place. Sandy's hand action was building him up rather quickly. It wouldn't be long. Tingles surged through his loins. His cock contracted a couple of times, then spewed forth wad after thick wad of white cum. It splashed all over his chest and abs and he finished with a loud grunt of relief.

Sandy grinned and kissed him. "Bet you weren't expecting this tonight."

Jimmy shook his head, looked from Sandy to Moira and back again. "Did you two plan this."

Both Moira and Sandy exchanged a knowing glance, and Moira said, "What do you think?"